THE SEASON FINALE

PARANORMAL TALENT AGENCY

EPISODE SIX

HEATHER SILVIO

Panther Books

Published in the United States by Panther Books, Las Vegas.

Correspondence to the author may be sent to:
heather@heathersilvio.com

Cover design by Sonia Freitas at Chloe Belle Arts
https://ChloeBelleArts.com

ISBN (Print) 978-1-7326938-9-0
ISBN (E-book) 978-1-951192-00-6

ACKNOWLEDGMENTS

Thank you to the readers who came along for this ride.

CHAPTER ONE

Television reporters get used to being eyed with suspicion, but usually, those doing the eyeing are human. Not this time. I didn't think. The attractive man had stared at me the moment I entered the café. *Soprannaturale*, where all the nonhumans hung out. I glanced around at the framed pictures of pastoral Italian scenes and classic checkered tablecloths on two-tops scattered throughout the front of the café. Stepping closer to the man, the scent of flowers and earth reached me.

"You smell sweet," I blurted out. "Is that some kind of cologne, or an essential oil you're diffusing?"

The man's eyes widened, then narrowed. "May I help you?"

Refusing to be thrown by his non-response to my question, I smiled wide and extended my hand. "Elizabeth Addison, reporter," I introduced myself, smile faltering when he hesitated. An imperceptible sigh and then his large hand engulfed my smaller one. Breath caught in my throat at the tingles that raced through my body. I snatched my hand back and he smirked.

"Antonio DiMaio. Owner of this fine establishment." His chocolate-brown eyes took in my appearance, a bit bedraggled due to a short rain. Contrary to the public perception of living in the desert, it rained in Las Vegas. And since it was spring, well, it had rained while I walked from my car to the door of his fine establishment.

I attempted to smooth down my short, curly brown hair, frizzy from the humidity, and then ran my hands down the sides of my simple blue shift. Antonio's eyes followed the movement, the smirk morphing into something more complex.

His eyes snapped back up to mine. "May I help you, Ms. Addison?"

"Please, call me Liz," I responded by reflex.

"Then call me Tony."

I nodded. "Tony. I'm meeting Catherine Rodham. Do you know her?"

"Because all supernaturals know each other?" he asked, smirk back in place.

I flushed. "No." A smart retort didn't come to me, because now I wanted to know what type of creature he was. Given my instant attraction, I wondered if he was an incubus. I'd learned from Catherine last year that they could control you by sucking out your soul. Yuck. Though she swore her half-incubus boyfriend Alex didn't do that.

He chuckled, his rumbly voice sexy. "Relax. I'm just teasing you."

Was he *flirting* with me? His comment did not help me relax. If anything, my flush deepened. He ran a hand through his longish wavy black hair and smiled, a dimple appearing on his right cheek.

"But I do know Catherine," he admitted. "She isn't here yet."

"I'll wait for her before being seated." I took the opportunity while I waited to consider his sinewy muscles flexing underneath a simple black shirt and pants. Probably his work uniform. His appearance placed him maybe late-twenties like me, but with supernatural beings, who knew? I desperately wanted to ask what he was, but that had to be a faux pas.

"Did you have any questions?"

My eyes widened. Could he read minds?

"About the menu," he clarified, though I didn't miss the quick smile.

If he was going to flirt with me, then I would be bold. "I do have a question." Our eyes met. "Not about the menu."

He tilted his head. "Ask away."

"What are you?"

"Not fully human."

I shook my head. "That's entirely unhelpful."

"I know."

"Are you flirting with me?"

His eyebrows lifted in surprise. "Do you want me to flirt with you?"

My mouth dropped open, but nothing emerged.

He laughed. "I like you, little human."

I bristled.

He held up his hands in surrender. "It's a term of endearment where I come from."

"Where are you from?"

"Originally Italy."

"When was that, Tony?"

"Nice try, Liz."

"It was worth the shot."

"I have a question for you," he said.

"I'm fully human."

Tony threw back his head and belly laughed. "That's not in doubt."

"How would you know?"

"I know."

"That's mysterious."

He smiled. "As a human," he started, "how did you even know about my café?"

A voice answered from behind me. "I'd like to know that as well."

CHAPTER TWO

"Catherine, thanks for meeting me here," I responded. Hmm, she wasn't alone. Mia Fynn stood to the side of the tall, blond talent agent. "Hi, Mia."

She smiled uncertainly, her bright green eyes wary. "Hi, Liz."

Mia and I had even more history than Catherine and I did; we'd worked together to solve a series of murders, and it turned out to be a crazy djinn (that's a genie to most humans). I'm not sure why they were surprised when I put being a reporter first. It was my job. That's what I did. Still, I knew they felt betrayed that I played an instrumental role in exposing the paranormal underworld at the end of last year. In my defense, we all later learned that this was a good thing. *Why* it was good was part of my current mission.

"Barbara Knollman told me about the café," I explained to the three of them. The new mayor had turned out to be a former demon, current angel, head of both the human city council and the paranormal underworld. That had all blown my mind when I learned it last week. And, then when Barbara made her request… well, that's why I was here. I turned to face the dreamy café owner. Wait, dreamy? No way was I getting involved with a supernatural. I don't care how good looking and flirtatious he was.

"I guess we'll need a table for three," I told Tony.

"Right this way." The three of us followed Tony to the back of the café. I tried and failed not to appreciate his rear assets. My eyes rolled of their own accord at my ridiculousness. We sat in the green vinyl-covered booth he indicated. When my eyes met his, he waggled his eyebrows at me. Did he know I was checking him out? How? Now my reporter-sense was twitching. I'd find out what manner of supernatural he was eventually. Right now, I had more important matters. I finger waved goodbye at Tony and he sauntered away.

"Not that it isn't good to see you, Mia, but why are you here?" I asked bluntly.

Mia laughed her tinkling laugh, shaking her head, green hair moving with the motion. She was a nixie, kind of like a mermaid, though don't tell her that, and could bewitch people with her voice. I knew that firsthand. "Catherine doesn't trust you," she answered and I flushed.

"I was just doing my job."

Catherine held up a hand to stop us from continuing. "It doesn't matter. Why did you want to meet with me, Liz?" Genuine curiosity shown in her blue eyes, so I hoped the truth would pull her in. I knew better than to lie. She was a natural lie detector; I guess you could call that her superpower.

"You saw the interview I conducted with Barbara last week?" Two heads nodded in response. "After the interview, Barbara asked for my help with an investigation." Catherine's expression became more guarded. "She wants me to investigate you, Catherine."

The object of my investigation sighed and Mia glanced at her quizzically. "She's telling the truth," Catherine told Mia. Guess her lie detector could tell I wasn't being deceitful. Catherine held my gaze. "Barbara has hinted that I'm somehow involved with the supernatural underworld since I moved to Vegas last year to start the talent agency."

"You have no idea why?"

"No." I heard the frustration in her voice. "Trust me, I'd love to know. A lot of stuff happened that might have been avoided if I knew." Her expression turned thoughtful. "Barbara still doesn't know? Even though she's been elevated to an angel again?"

I shrugged. "Apparently not. She said you're the key to something big. That's what she wants me to investigate."

"Why you?" Mia asked and I tensed, but her body and expression remained open. That wasn't a dig at me.

"Maybe because I've been covering this story from the beginning?" I laughed. "She did mention my awesome *Mythological Being of the Week* segment on *Entertainment Daily.*" I hosted the top-rated entertainment morning show in Las Vegas, and once I unearthed some paranormal secrets, I had found my calling. Audiences ate it up.

Catherine rolled her eyes. "Yeah, that's a great segment."

"Sarcasm?"

"Of course not."

We stared at each other for a beat before she sighed again. "I know you're telling the truth. I want to know what's going on, too. So, I guess we can work together." She bit her lower lip, but I grinned. She might not be happy, but it thrilled me to be on the front line of another paranormal scoop.

"You'll help, too?" Catherine asked Mia, who was already shaking her head.

"I'd love to, Catherine, you know that. But I have a new movie going into production—"

"Say no more," Catherine interrupted her. "If you say I can trust Liz enough—"

"Hey!" This time I cut Catherine off. "No need to be rude."

"I wasn't being rude, Liz."

Mia giggled and a sense of calm wrapped the table.

"Watch it with the bewitching," I warned the nixie.

"Sorry," she said, though did not seem sorry. "I didn't want you guys to get off track." She stared at Catherine. "You'll know if she's lying. I wouldn't worry about it."

"True."

I clapped my hands in delight and the women smiled. "This will be exciting. I can't wait to find out what the heck makes you so important." I mean, yes, she knew if someone was telling the truth or not, but she didn't have *real* powers. I didn't think. Hmm.

The ladies distracted my wandering thoughts by exiting the booth. I hurried to join them.

"I wish you both luck," Mia said. "Please let me know if I can do anything. I'll miss working with you on this."

A pang of regret hit me. We had fun investigating those murders. I genuinely liked Mia. And Catherine, I supposed, though I didn't know her as well. My mouth opened to respond, but thick white smoke filled the area before us.

Blocking the way out.

CHAPTER THREE

Fear filled me at the thought of being trapped in a fire, though my brain was already registering that I felt no heat and could still breathe. The smoke swirled and began to take shape.

"Are you guys seeing what I'm seeing?" Catherine whispered.

I nodded and heard a murmur of agreement from Mia. Noises from others in the café sounded distant somehow. Like there was a barrier between us and them. The smoke, maybe.

The smoke coalesced then cleared, leaving behind a woman. She seemed late twenties with average height and weight. She had long red hair and blue eyes. And wore a jumpsuit of some kind. A pantsuit? But like a onesie. My brain went on a mad scamper to identify her unusual outfit. Then her mouth opened and my brain froze.

"Stop," she whispered. Her wild gaze flicked between the three of us. Like she was trying to figure out who we were.

"Stop what?" Mia asked.

"Stop," the woman repeated. She appeared confused.

"Who are you?" I tried. Her eyes focused on me and then widened.

"Elizabeth Addison," she answered instead.

Something uncomfortable flared at the idea this woman who just appeared in the café knew who I was. "Yes," I confirmed. "Who are you?" I repeated my question.

"Stop the investigation."

My eyebrows lifted. "Stop what investigation?"

"When am I?" the woman asked instead, turning her head to take in her surroundings.

"Do you mean, where are you?" Catherine asked.

The woman lasered in on her. "Catherine Rodham."

In the periphery of my vision, I saw Catherine nod.

"When am I?" the woman repeated.

"April 5, 2019," I answered.

The woman blew out a frustrated breath. "I was hoping to stop your broadcast."

That was clearly directed at me. "Which broadcast?"

"I tried to get to you before the broadcast, but I timed it wrong," she continued like I hadn't spoken. She shrugged. "It's not an exact science."

"What's not?" I asked.

"Time travel."

Said so matter of fact, I almost believed I'd misheard. "Time travel?"

"When are you from?" Catherine asked. Guess her lie detector told her the woman was telling the truth – or at least believed she was. She did materialize out of thin air, so there was that.

"2219."

Silence greeted the date she provided, our brains processing the idea that the woman standing before us had traveled 200 years back in time. To get me to stop my broadcast. Of what? I zeroed back in on that, glad to give my brain something concrete to focus on.

"Which broadcast were you trying to stop? What story did you not want me to tell?"

The time traveler took a step toward me and it was all I could do not to flinch away. Her intensity was intimidating. "You need to stop investigating Catherine Rodham and you need to prevent the integration of the paranormal and human societies."

A nervous laugh bubbled up. "Oh, is that all?"

The woman frowned. "This is a joke?" Her eyes flashed and now I did take a step back.

"No, it's not a joke," Mia jumped in, attempting to smooth things over.

"Your bewitching will not work on me," the woman informed Mia.

"Who are you?" I asked. This was ridiculous. She was crazy or a paranormal, or both, but it was time to figure that out.

"My name is Rowan Walsh and I died in the year 2219."

Catherine, Mia, and I exchanged startled glances.

"I'm sorry," Catherine said, "did you just say you *died* in the year 2219?"

The woman nodded.

"You're not just a time traveler, but a time traveling ghost?" My question squeaked out. This meeting had taken a very unexpected turn.

The woman, Rowan, nodded again.

"And you're here to stop us from figuring me out—" Catherine began.

"Yes," Rowan interrupted.

"And to keep Barbara from integrating human and paranormal societies?" I finished Catherine's summary question.

"Yes."

"Why?" The reporter in me wasn't about to stop investigating on the say-so of an alleged time traveling ghost. I mean, really.

"If you don't, many people will die."

"Oh." Hmm, many people dying wasn't so good. "Are you sure?"

Rowan's blue eyes flashed again, hard like ice, and I shivered. "Yes."

I waited for her to provide details and when she did not, I risked a quick glance at Catherine and Mia. They seemed as much at a loss as I felt.

Screw that. "Rowan, ma'am," I started with a sugary-sweet voice. "I appreciate that you believe all of this to be true. However, it's my job to investigate newsworthy events and people." I held up a hand to stop her from interrupting. "And, frankly, I have nothing to do with what Mayor Barbara Knollman does or does not do with respect to paranormal-human integration." I stopped to gauge her reaction, proud that my voice didn't waver in the slightest.

"That is your final answer?"

"What *is* this, a game show?" I quipped in response. Catherine or Mia gasped and Rowan's eyes flashed again.

"That is your final answer?" Rowan repeated.

"Yes, it is," I stated. "I will not stop investigating based on a vague statement from an alleged time-traveling ghost."

"Are you sure that's a good idea, Liz?" Mia asked.

"Yeah, maybe we should think about this," Catherine added. "After all, I'm the object of the investigation."

I shook my head. "It's my final answer," I said to Rowan.

"If you stay on this path, you will die in three days," she responded.

"Did you just threaten me?" My voice rose an octave.

"I speak the truth."

"Liz, we should talk about this," Mia insisted.

Against my instincts and better judgment, I took a step toward Rowan and chuckled. "Just checking, but does today count as day one or zero?"

CHAPTER FOUR

Smoke formed around Rowan, obscuring her. We watched, waiting to see what would happen next. When the white smoke cleared, the time traveling ghost was gone. The first eyes I met were Tony's, and he appeared confused. He stepped from behind the takeout counter and approached.

"Can any of you tell me what just happened?"

"What did you see?" I asked instead, curious what was visible beyond the smoke we had seen.

He furrowed his brow. "It all happened so fast. I could see the three of you sitting at the booth. Then you… blurred, I guess is the best word… and when it cleared you were standing here in front of the booth instead. You moved in the blink of an eye."

"Interesting," I muttered.

"That's all I get," he responded, but he smiled.

I laughed. "It lasted longer than a blink of an eye. You missed Rowan, the time traveling ghost."

His mouth dropped open. "I'm sorry, what?"

I explained what had happened behind the blurring he saw – apparently of time and space, how weird was that?

"Well, then, you have to stop investigating Catherine. And, you should probably talk to the mayor about her plans, too," Tony concluded.

I arched an eyebrow. "I appreciate the concern, but that isn't going to happen."

"Is any investigation worth your life?"

I touched his arm, shocked by the thrill that raced through me again. "You just met me, but trust me when I say this. Nobody scares me off a story."

"I don't know," Catherine interjected. "It's not just your life at risk, but countless lives in the future."

"Maybe. According to the woman who just popped in and out of existence," I argued, and glanced at Mia for support.

She shrugged. "I'm not sure. I've been around hundreds of years. It's not as long as you think."

"Okay, playing devil's advocate," Catherine began, "how certain are we that she's from the future?"

"She was wearing the typical *Star Trek* onesie-type outfit," I offered with a smirk.

Tony laughed at my joke, before catching himself with a scowl. Wow, he was really concerned about my safety.

"In all seriousness, I am curious about Rowan and what she said, but there's no way to verify anything. I'm not prepared to stop what I'm doing – or ask Barbara to do the same – on unverifiable information." I looked at their faces; surely someone would see the logic of my argument and support me.

Mia was wavering. She narrowed her eyes in thought. "I suppose we could do some research on anybody named Rowan Walsh, both on the internet and in the magical community."

"Now we're talking," I crowed, glad to have some support.

"I'm not sure how successful we'll be, though, if she's telling the truth about being from the future," Mia warned.

"That's okay, at least we're trying something," I insisted.

"She didn't say she agreed that you should continue the investigation," Tony argued.

I turned to Catherine. "You're the Chosen One, right? Can't you just save me from Rowan, if it comes down to it?"

Catherine fidgeted. "I guess so?"

I chuckled. "I'm just giving you a hard time." I faced the group. "I don't know what will happen, or not. But I don't want to change what I'm doing on the say-so of someone who could simply be a deranged supernatural being. It's not like we haven't seen those before," I added drily.

"She's right," came a familiar voice. We all turned toward the back of the café where the sound originated.

CHAPTER FIVE

A blue-haired, blue-eyed being stood near the hallway leading to the bathrooms and the kitchen. She smiled an ethereal smile as she gazed upon us. I hadn't met her before, but based on Barbara Knollman's description, I knew who she was.

"Please correct me if I'm wrong," I turned to the group, waving my arm in a flourish, "but I believe this is Olivia Williams, archangel extraordinaire."

I had the mad thought of wondering whether she considered us like ants, scurrying, helpful, but ultimately squishable. She turned her magnetic blue eyes on me and I squirmed. I didn't think the archangel could read minds, but who knew?

"We've met," she responded, her voice smooth and velvety. "Hi, Catherine, Mia." She extended a hand to Tony. "You're new."

"Tony," he said, hesitating before grasping her hand. Her blue eyes twinkled at the hesitation.

"It's good you're here, since you're one of the beings who keeps saying I'm so important to the supernatural world. Right?" Catherine challenged the archangel.

Olivia lifted her hands. "I only know what I know," she responded cryptically.

"I'm an empath, nobody special," Catherine argued. "And now, Liz's life and untold people's lives in the future are at risk. Because of me." Her voice thickened with unshed tears and I startled. I had no idea she was this upset.

Olivia placed her hands onto Catherine's shoulders. "You are so much more than you think."

"Wouldn't it be easier if you just told us?" I asked with a sigh.

Olivia wrinkled her nose at me. "Liz, isn't this what you live for? Investigating? Would you really want me to tell you all the answers?"

Her questions stumped me.

"Are you kidding right now?" Catherine asked in exasperation. "No offense, Liz, but if Olivia can give us the answers, I, for one, want them."

I reddened. "Of course, if it can save lives…"

"Unfortunately, it truly doesn't work that way," Olivia said.

"Why not?" Catherine refused to let it go.

Olivia shrugged. "That's not how the universe works."

"The universe works in mysterious ways," I offered with a wink.

"That's not quite what I mean, but that'll do," Olivia concurred.

"Even if it can help us save lives," Catherine said incredulously.

"Catherine, maybe Olivia isn't able to provide the answers we want," Mia soothed.

"Then why are you here?" I asked, not rancorously but out of genuine curiosity.

The archangel laughed. "Changing timelines suggested that you might choose not to continue on this path."

Gasps sounded at the statement, and even I was flummoxed. "Changing timelines? Is Rowan a time-traveling ghost?"

"I'm here to remind you that things are not always as they appear."

"That's not terribly helpful," I responded and Olivia frowned at me. My insides quivered.

"My goal in life is to be helpful, Liz."

"Point taken."

Olivia glanced around before continuing. "It's important you don't lose sight of your goals: investigating Catherine and supporting Barbara's initiatives."

Tony, who'd been silent to this point, chimed in. "I'm with Catherine on this one. Is it worth all these lives to push forward with the investigation?"

Olivia put her hands on her hips and glared at us like we were recalcitrant children. I guess even archangels can get fed up. "This is your choice. Remember though that you do not know what will happen if you choose not to go down this path. It may be worse." Her pronouncement made, she vanished.

"I hadn't thought about that," Catherine acknowledged.

Mia shook her head. "That's probably why Olivia can't tell us much. If we believe that nothing is set in the timeline – or even that there are multiple timelines – anything she tells us could irrevocably change what will happen. Including for the worse."

"What if what she told us made things better?" Catherine argued, but I could see her heart wasn't in it anymore.

"We could talk in circles around this, scientifically, philosophically, whatever. It doesn't matter. We aren't getting additional information from Olivia, or anyone else." I gulped a huge breath of air. "We need to decide what we're going to do."

Thick white smoke swirled before us.

"Oh, no. Not again," I grumbled.

CHAPTER SIX

Rowan glared at us when the smoke cleared. "What are you doing?"

"Talking," I responded.

"The timeline is doing weird things."

"How's that our fault?"

"I'm trying to save my husband and children," she raged.

That threw me. "Oh."

"Oh? That's it."

Indecision wracked me for a moment. "We've been told that your timeline isn't set. Stopping progress won't have the outcome you want." If only I was as confident as I sounded.

Rowan threw up her hands. "If this is the way you want it to be."

"Wait," Mia interjected. "What does that mean?"

"What are you planning on doing?" Catherine asked.

"I gave you the opportunity to make the right decision—"

"According to you," I interrupted. She clenched her fists and I smiled. I never did learn when to back down, or when not to poke the beast.

Rowan appeared confused. "The timeline started to…" She stopped and stared again.

"Started to what?" I asked.

"It doesn't matter. I need to know right now whether or not you are continuing the investigation," she demanded.

Her tone rankled. "I'll take the risk to my life."

"You refuse to stop?"

"As I said before, I refuse to back down. I am a journalist," I declared, a bit pompously, truth be told. "Threats will never stop me." I sensed movement and glanced to my side in time to catch the end of Mia's eye roll.

Rowan lifted her hands above her and closed her eyes. I exchanged uneasy glances with Catherine, Mia, and Tony.

"What is she doing?" Tony asked.

"I don't know," I admitted, bracing myself for what would be coming. Whatever that was.

The tips of Rowan's fingers crackled with energy. She swung around, directing this energy to the café bar. What looked like red lightning jumped from her fingertips to shatter the glass cases. I flinched, throwing my hands up in front of my face, even though the glass would likely never fly that far. The scent of ozone filled the air.

Rowan flickered in and out, like an image being turned off and on, as she became increasingly translucent.

"She's using up her energy," Mia shouted.

Rowan solidified and turned toward Mia.

"Not fast enough," I responded.

Rowan's eyes were lit up from behind, like a candle had been lit inside her skull. She lifted her hands toward the ceiling again. That red energy moved across her fingertips.

"Behind the booth," Tony shouted, and we flung ourselves in that direction. Rowan lowered her hands toward us. Red lightning arced from her. The booth's table fractured and tendrils of smoke rose where the wood burned.

I met Catherine's wide eyes on the other side of the booth. We were smushed up against the bottom of the booth's seats, trying to stay out of the line of fire. "It'll be okay," I yelled to her.

"No, it won't," Rowan roared. She'd stepped closer and stood mere feet from where we cowered.

Energy flowed nearby, drawing my attention. A glance at Catherine and my jaw dropped open. Her eyes looked like Rowan's, lit up from behind. She faded in and out, becoming translucent and then opaque.

"What the—"

Rowan's cry cut off my words. "You will stop or you will die!" Flickering in and out like a flashlight with a dying battery, probably an accurate analogy, she shot off one last stream of lightning. The energy landed where Catherine was. My heart leapt into my throat – until I realized I could see through the talent agent. Her eyes closed.

"Catherine!" I yelled.

Silence filled the café. That scent of ozone crowded out all other smells. Rowan was gone. Catherine had solidified again and lay curled on her side next to a large splintered piece of the table. Tony rose from behind the booth's back, assisting Mia up. She had a nasty bruise forming over her right eye.

I scuttled forward to grab Catherine. I tilted her head up, heaved a sigh of relief when I saw she was breathing. "Catherine? Can you hear me?"

Tony and Mia stumbled around the remains of the booth and joined me beside Catherine.

"Is she okay?" Mia asked.

"Catherine," I repeated. "Can you hear me?"

"Wha—" she mumbled, then stopped. Her eyes fluttered open. "Is everybody okay?" she rasped out.

"Thankfully, yes," Mia answered.

Tony helped Catherine to her feet. Mia and I followed them to a couple of two-top tables. The café had emptied during the attack. That seemed for the best; no collateral damage.

The four of us collapsed into chairs and stared at each other. "That was exciting," I said with a crooked smile.

Mia laughed, as always sounding like tinkling bells. Tony shook his head, but I saw the corners of his eyes crinkle with a half-smile.

Catherine still looked shell-shocked. "I thought you had three days. Rowan attacked us."

"Yes," I confirmed.

She stared at me. "You have to stop the investigation."

"No."

"Catherine's right," Tony argued.

"No."

"Is there anything we can say to change your mind?" Mia questioned.

"No."

"What if I refuse to cooperate?"

"It wouldn't matter, Catherine," I answered softly. "Based on everything we've seen and heard, although my head wants to explode thinking about it, there are multiple possible timelines, and the archangel says we shouldn't stray from the path." I shook my head to stop any of them from interrupting. "Besides, now we have an even bigger question to answer. Though I suppose it's just an offshoot of the original investigation," I mumbled, more to myself than to them.

"What bigger question could there be besides determining Catherine's role in all of this?" Mia asked.

I placed my hands palms-down on the table, sliding my fingers back and forth for a moment, before stilling. "Did anyone besides me see Catherine phase in and out? Just like the ghost."

CHAPTER SEVEN

"What are you talking about, Liz? I didn't phase in and out of anything," Catherine protested. She looked at Tony and Mia for support.

"We were behind the booth," Mia admitted, "so we didn't see anything."

"What do you mean, she phased in and out like the ghost?" Tony asked me.

"Did you guys see Rowan phasing in and out?" I asked in response.

Mia nodded and Tony answered, "She flickered, yes."

"And you saw the way her eyes lit up?" They nodded. "That's what Catherine did too."

Catherine shook her head. "No, there's no way."

"How did you feel during the attack?" I asked.

Catherine suddenly became interested in her cuticles. "I don't know."

"Yes, you do," I pressured.

She gripped the side of the chair and looked between the three of us. "Okay, I felt weird."

"Weird in what way?" I pushed more.

Catherine frowned. "I can't describe it too much more than that." She brightened. "Actually, that's not true. My eyes felt hot. Burning. Sounds and smells faded in and out."

"That would make sense," I said, thinking it through.

"What would?" Mia asked.

"The light from her eyes, whatever it is, must be some form of energy; thus, accounting for the burning sensation. And, the flickering… if Catherine was phasing in and out of our timeline—" I held up a hand to forestall questions I couldn't answer. "—which is only a guess, then it's logical that her senses would do the same."

Catherine snorted. "Logical. As if any of this could be called that."

I laughed. "No doubt." I sobered quickly. "But I don't think I'm wrong. I think Catherine phased in and out of our timeline, our existence, whatever you want to call it."

Catherine had gone an unhealthy shade of white. "What does that mean?"

"I have no idea. Except that there isn't any chance, in this timeline or any others, that I'm stopping the investigation now. Not when it's gotten so interesting."

Mia rolled her eyes again; she really needed to stop

doing that. I wondered what it was about me that seemed to trigger it. I focused on her when I realized she was talking. "—support Liz."

"Wait, did you just say that you support me?"

"Yes, Liz." She smiled at me and then turned a half-frown at Catherine. "I don't understand why you're so important. But, you're clearly more than an empath. And, regardless of the concerns that Rowan has expressed… and trust me, I have my own concerns about the future repercussions… the bottom line is I agree with Liz that we need to help you figure out who—"

"Or what," Catherine corrected with a one-shoulder shrug.

Mia nodded. "—or what you are."

Tony sighed. "I'm not happy lives are at risk." He met my gaze. The frank fear there startled me. "But I agree with Liz and Mia. Catherine, you need to figure this out. And, Liz is right that you don't know that not taking action will help the timeline. Plus, the archangel said to keep going."

Catherine held up her hands in surrender. "Okay, okay, you've convinced me. What do we do first?"

"Mia has professional engagements, so she's out," I said.

"I can get coverage if you guys need my help," Mia offered. "I'd hate for you to be short-handed."

Catherine patted her on the arm. "That's not necessary. You and Liz got the serial killing genie. Now it's my turn."

"And, Tony is going to need to repair the damage to his café, so he'll be a less active partner, too," I continued. "Sorry about that, by the way." He shook his head with a laugh and reached out to squeeze my hand resting on the table. My eyes widened at the tingle his touch elicited; he smiled wolfishly in response.

"You'll make it up to me," he replied.

"Mmm, okay," I mumbled. Mia bit back a laugh and glanced knowingly in my direction. My face flushed and I broke eye contact with Tony. We could deal with our attraction later.

"In all seriousness, though, if you need any help, please ask," he added.

"We will," Catherine assured him.

"That leaves me and Catherine," I concluded. "Which is fine. I have several ideas."

"They are…?" Catherine prompted.

"Tomorrow morning, on-air, we launch the investigation."

"Shouldn't we discuss your plans first?" Catherine asked.

"And give you a chance to try to talk me out of it? Not at all."

"Fair enough," Catherine said.

"What are you planning to say?" Mia asked.

I smiled a Cheshire-cat grin. "You'll have to tune in to find out."

CHAPTER EIGHT

"Okay, spill it," Marilyn ordered. She narrowed her purple eyes (contacts, I always assumed) at me when she delivered the request.

"What do you mean?" I asked, failing, I'm sure, to maintain an innocent air.

"Close your eyes."

I obeyed, and her voice moved closer when she leaned in to work. A brush feathered shadow across one eyelid and then the other. "What story are you doing this morning that they bumped your original story?"

"You'll get to see soon, along with everyone else," I teased her, careful not to move, lest she draw a line across my face. Her tsk-tsk at my failure to enlighten her elicited a chuckle.

"Open your eyes."

I complied, and she cemented my face into place.

Marilyn sighed. "Okay, you're done. Pain in my butt." She glared a final moment, but a wink belied the words and tone. She ran a hand through her spiky platinum blond hair before turning to leave. "This better be worth it."

"It will be," I called after her. In truth, nerves fluttered more than I was letting on. While it was true I had joined Mia last year in tracking down a serial killer who had turned out to be a deadly supernatural being, I personally had never been targeted before. It unnerved me to know that Rowan directed her threat at me. Of course, I still didn't even know if she meant she'd kill me, or if my death would be a consequence of continuing the investigation.

I furrowed my brow and watched the brunette in the mirror mimic me. I smiled, pleased that my lipstick was even and no stains appeared on my front teeth. I stood, smoothing one hand down my bright pink sheath and the other down a single short flyaway curl.

A head appeared in the doorway of my dressing room. She opened her mouth but stopped when she saw me.

"I'm on my way," I informed the production assistant. She nodded and her head withdrew. A final glance at my flawless appearance in the mirror, a reminder to the butterflies in my stomach that this would be helpful, and an exaggerated wink at the newscaster in the mirror. It was show time.

"Good morning in the Valley," I greeted viewers to my morning show, *Entertainment Daily*. "Thank you for spending your morning with us." I perched on a cushy blue chair, legs crossed at the ankles, knees kept together. Demure, yet with my pink stiletto heels, sexy. I loved this combination. The camera closest to me lowered into position and I allowed my smile to slip.

"This morning we start with a story that isn't uplifting and fun, that isn't so positive." I took a deep breath. "Yesterday, a supernatural being told me I would die in three days." I ignored the gasps I heard from the production staff; this was partly why I didn't tell anybody ahead of time what I would be saying. It was a good thing I had such a strong relationship with our producer. I shifted toward another camera. Needlessly dramatic, to be honest, but the public expected it.

"Today is Day Two." Continuing to ignore additional gasps and whispered comments, I explained to the viewers about Rowan's visit to *Soprannaturale*, though I chose not to name the café. This next part would be trickiest; to ask for assistance without throwing a spotlight on Catherine. I didn't care about it being on me. Heck, as a media personality, I loved it. But as it stood, she barely agreed to this investigation.

"According to this time-traveling ghost, I'm slated to die tomorrow. Not if I can help it," I assured my viewers, pleased to hear the steel in my voice.

"Today I ask you for help. There is a woman in town. She is human, but with supernatural abilities. Possibly much more than she ever thought. I am seeking additional information about her." I held up a hand. "Before anyone asks, I'm not divulging her name. Now, I can practically hear some of you asking, How do I know if I know anything about her if I don't know her name?" I smiled and nodded. "Trust me, she's impacting the supernatural energy in Las Vegas. If you have sensed something, seen something, whatever, please get in touch with me. My email is below on the screen, or you can go to our website to access it there. I'm just a human, asking the supernatural world for help. Help me help this woman, and maybe save my life in the process. Thank you." I gave a final smile without showing teeth and waited for the director to indicate the live feed stopped.

I stood, wavered slightly, reached a hand out to steady myself. A blur of well-wishes reached my ears. I nodded in response to words I wasn't truly hearing during the walk back to my office. The ringing of the telephone greeted me before I had taken a seat behind my utilitarian desk. I kept my gaze on my desk, for the first time wishing I didn't have floor-to-ceiling glass surrounding my office. Today it felt way too much like a fishbowl. A different ring cut through the office phone ring. I snatched my cell out of my top drawer.

"Elizabeth Addison," I identified myself when I didn't recognize the number, though it was a Vegas area code.

"Liz?"

I recognized the voice. "Robin?" She and I hadn't had the best relationship, but in the last month or so, she'd broken her blood vow as a demon's minion and rediscovered her witch's magic. She could be a powerful ally – and source of information.

CHAPTER NINE

Blood thrummed through my body and my heart rate beat a fast pitter-patter. But this was excitement, not nervousness. Catherine and I were about to have an audience with the Witches Council.

Did they call it an audience? My knowledge of protocol was sorely lacking. Good thing Robin had issued the invitation.

The witch stood beside us outside the large, squat, metal-gray building off of Industrial Road. She pulled on the end of her brunette ponytail, her brown eyes staring straight ahead.

"Are you ready?" Robin pulled the door open before we even answered her question.

"Yes," I answered anyway. Catherine didn't move. I tugged on her arm. "Hey, are you coming?"

She fixed her unfocused expression on me.

"Is everything okay?" I mean, she was somehow connected to the possible deaths of untold people in the future. But still. This seemed different.

Catherine offered a low wattage smile. "I'm coming."

Robin led us across the linoleum floor, past several hard, plastic chairs, to an unassuming door at the back wall. She rapped her knuckles three times. Within seconds, the door opened to reveal a stunning redhead with a big smile and brown eyes. She enveloped Robin in a hug before addressing me and Catherine.

"Hi, Elizabeth, I'm Jessica. I recognize you from your show," Jessica gushed.

"Call me Liz," I responded.

"Liz. And you must be Catherine."

Catherine nodded though stayed silent.

"Thank you so much for agreeing to see us," I said. "It seemed your area of expertise."

"When we saw your broadcast…" Her smile faltered. "Anything we can do to help you both." She turned, calling over her shoulder. "Please, follow me."

Robin, Catherine, and I followed Jessica down a short hallway. She knocked twice on a door on the left, then eased it open for us to enter.

I gasped at the antique wall sconces and silvery wallpaper that reflected the light.

Jessica glanced back at me with a smile. "We wanted a lovely workplace."

"You succeeded." I almost laughed when I realized I was whispering. The soft gray carpeting kept our steps silent; the overall effect was like a library.

Jessica pointed to folding chairs arranged before a half-circle table with five office chairs opposite. "Have a seat. The others are on their way."

Robin, Catherine, and I sat in the folding chairs; the cushioned seats meant they were much more comfortable than I had guessed. Jessica took a seat at one end of the other set of chairs. I had just wondered how long we'd have to wait when a door behind those chairs squeaked open. Several people filed in. As they sat, Jessica introduced them and they gave smiles or waves.

"This is Theresa," indicating a middle-aged blond with bright purple lipstick.

"Matt," an older bald gentleman.

"Evan," a taller, heavyset man.

"And, last but not least, Marcie," a young blond woman.

When all five council members were seated, Jessica faced us with a blinding smile. "Welcome to the Witches Council. Let's get started. What can we do to help?"

Robin and Catherine looked at me. Guess I was taking point. I stood to address the council. That seemed respectful; maybe they should publish a handbook so people knew what to do. Did the royal family do that?

I focused on the council. "We understand that you watched my broadcast this morning." The councilmembers nodded. "Let me give you the background." I updated them on what had happened since Rowan made her appearance yesterday. Had it only been one day? "As I stated in the broadcast, I die tomorrow if Rowan is to be believed. I'd really rather not," I added with a half-smile. Low chuckles sounded. Some of the tension in the room released.

"We are approaching you to ask if you can provide any information about the time-traveling ghost who calls herself Rowan Walsh; anything about Catherine's role in this; and anything about concerns regarding Mayor Barbara Knollman's plans for integrating the human and supernatural communities." I ticked these off on my fingers.

"You don't ask for much," Evan responded drily.

"I'm a journalist. It's what I do."

"Indeed," he conceded. He turned to Matt. "What have we learned?"

Matt cleared his throat. "After seeing your broadcast, we did some exploring."

"Exploring?" Catherine asked.

Theresa nodded. "Matt, if you don't mind?"

"Please."

Theresa closed her eyes. "My abilities involve an acute sensitivity to fluctuations in the magical energy of the city."

"You can feel changes in the Force?" I joked. She opened her eyes then frowned.

"Liz." Catherine chastised me with the single word.

"Sorry," I mumbled.

"Yesterday, there was a significant fluctuation," Theresa continued. "Unlike any I had felt before."

A chill moved through me.

"There was a huge increase to start."

I opened my mouth to ask a question. Robin's hand on my arm stilled me.

Theresa shook her head. "Then the magical energy dropped back down." She puckered her purple lips in thought. "Finally, it spiked even higher. This is where it became interesting." Her face flushed with excitement. "I sensed two distinct energy signatures. The first was that foreign one that surged and then receded. But, the other one. I'd never felt anything like it. In my entire life," she emphasized.

Blood drained from my face. "What do you think that means?"

Theresa exchanged a glance with Marcie, the youngest-appearing witch on the council, before answering. "Our best guess? The first magical energy surge was Rowan Walsh arriving in our time. The decrease was when she attacked the café. That final surge was her recovery before vanishing..." She stopped with a look at Jessica, who considered Catherine.

"What? What else?" Catherine asked in a whisper.

"We think the larger surge was you," Jessica answered.

"How?" I asked before Catherine could.

Jessica shook her head. "We don't know."

Disappointment filled me. I wanted more.

"Catherine is definitely more than an empath. She clearly is connected to Rowan and most likely is as well to whatever Barbara has seen in her visions since last year. However, we honestly have no idea what or how." Jessica tilted her head for a moment. "To answer your questions. We believe Rowan Walsh likely is from another dimension or timeline, and could be from the future, though we haven't been able to confirm or exclude that conclusion. Catherine absolutely has powers that have either not fully expressed or that she is somehow repressing. And, we don't have any idea the role of Mayor Knollman's integration plans with any of it."

I exchanged glances with Robin and Catherine, could see my disappointment mirrored there.

"Our magic is only so powerful," Jessica said. "I'm sorry we weren't more helpful."

"This was great," I contradicted the redheaded witch, who appeared startled by my statement. "You confirmed we're on the right track and that Rowan isn't just a nutjob to ignore." I blanched. "Of course, that means her threat of my impending death must be taken seriously too. At least we have another day before… something happens."

"What will you do next?" Jessica asked.

"Lunch. Followed by a visit to the mayor's office."

CHAPTER TEN

Tony's gaze found mine the moment I entered his café. Heat suffused me and that knowing smile appeared on his face. Why was it that hot men always seemed to know the effect they had on women? Good grief. I removed my own goofy smile and pointedly turned to face my companions. If I could hear him, I imagined Tony chuckling in response to my action.

"The back booth is still unusable, but the one next to it is clean and available," Tony called out.

Robin thanked him and led us to the booth. I settled into the vinyl seat, choosing to sit so I faced the restrooms and not the front of the café. The damage from Rowan's last visit was still very much in evidence. Someone had cleaned, but the back booth was split in two, the table missing a jagged chunk, and black marred the walls. Smoke? I didn't think it had been that bad.

The three of us perused the menu and ordered veggie sandwiches on ciabatta bread when the waitress came over.

"Is it too early for a cocktail?" Robin joked.

"It's five o'clock somewhere in the world," I responded. We laughed, Catherine a half second behind. "Catherine, you've been distracted all afternoon. What's going on?"

Catherine's wild eyes moved between us, a weird combination of excited and terrified. She opened her mouth, closed it. Flexed the fingers on both hands. Finally, took a quick breath. "Alex proposed."

"Congratulations," Robin enthused.

"Is this what you want?" I asked, playing the killjoy in the conversation. A sensation of being watched returned, and I peered around the edge of the booth to find Tony staring, a peculiar expression on his face.

"I don't know," Catherine answered me.

"Do you love him?" Robin asked.

Catherine smiled, her eyes taking on a faraway look for a moment. "Yes."

I sighed. Could she look more like the stereotype of a woman in love?

"What's the issue then?" Robin asked.

"It's because he's not human, right?" I answered instead and Catherine nodded, eyes filling with tears.

Robin placed her hand over Catherine's on the tabletop. "All relationships have challenges. But, nobody at this table is fully human."

"Speak for yourself," I retorted and then flushed. "That didn't come out quite the way I intended."

Robin shook her head. "It's okay, Liz. We know what you meant."

"Liz is right, though," Catherine said. "Dating a half-incubus is one thing. Marrying a half-incubus is another. I know I'm an empath, and something more, but still…" She frowned. "He's immortal and I'm not. It wouldn't be right for him to give that up – if it's even possible. Does he want to watch me grow old and die? What about me? It's selfish, but how will I feel as I age and he doesn't? Will I resent him his eternal good looks and immortality?" She took a deep breath, stopped the rapid-fire questions. "What should I do?"

"Catherine, you know we can't tell you what to do," Robin answered.

"I'll just play devil's advocate a bit longer," I chimed in.

"Of course, you will," Robin said.

"Can a human and a paranormal have a happily ever after? I think that's the big question," I started, but Robin interrupted.

"Can two paranormals have a happily ever after? Can two humans have a happily ever after? It's the same no matter their persuasion," she concluded.

"It adds an unnecessary complication," I argued.

"Could this be because of a certain supernatural?" Robin teased.

"What? No. I don't know what you're talking about," I stammered.

"Ladies," a deep voice addressed us and my body zinged in response. I looked up and found Tony's warm brown eyes, smelled his earthy scent, and wanted to run my fingers through his black hair. His smile widened. I didn't know what supernatural being he was, but I increasingly believed it was one that could read minds.

Tony set our sandwiches on the table. A chorus of thank-yous sounded. He shifted from foot to foot. Was he nervous? I tilted my head. "Was there something else?"

"Would you like to have dinner with me?"

Catherine bit off a laugh, but Robin didn't bother to hide her grin.

"No," I responded without thought, startled by the question.

My response didn't seem to faze him. "Because you don't think we have a future?"

One eyebrow rose in question. "How do you know that? Is this table bugged?"

"I have excellent hearing," he answered and wagged his ears at me.

"How did you do that?"

"I have skills."

"I bet." My ears burned at the double entendre. Tony smirked. An idea hit me. I mirrored his smirk, satisfied when his dropped a notch. "Yes, I'll go out with you—"

"Wonderful," he interrupted.

I held up a finger for him to wait. "I'll go out with you on one condition."

"Name it."

"Really? That could be dangerous. You don't know how my mind works."

"I'm getting an inkling."

"I'll go out with you if you tell me what you are." I sat back, pleased with my creativity. Robin choked on her water. Catherine's eyes widened. But Tony's smile broadened.

"You have a deal. Meet me at Fleming's on West Charleston for dinner at 7 and I'll tell you. You're not a vegetarian, right?"

"Um, no." I vaguely remembered that Fleming's was a steakhouse.

"See you tonight." He sauntered back to the café's bar, somehow no doubt aware of my appreciation of the view.

"That was different," Robin said.

"What do you mean?" I asked, shooting a look at Catherine when she laughed.

Robin held up her hands. "Don't get defensive. I've never seen him ask anyone out before. That's all I'm saying."

Hmm. I pushed that thought from my mind and focused. "Finish eating so we can head to Barbara Knollman's office."

I hoped the angel-turned-demon-turned-angel would have something useful to provide.

CHAPTER ELEVEN

I wanted to drive to the mayor's office, but since my Audi R8 didn't have a backseat to speak of, Robin drove us in her black VW Jetta compact sedan. It rode well, I could admit, but nothing beat being behind the wheel of my vehicle.

But I digress.

Mayor Knollman's secretary admitted us to the swanky office overlooking Main Street. Barbara stood when we entered. Her smile lit her face. Since being… elevated, I thought the word was, back to angel-status, she had regained an ethereal beauty. She no longer pulled her brunette hair back in a severe bun, her teeth no longer appeared small and sharp, and her fingernails no longer looked like talons. Plus, she looked decades younger. Turned out angels were much more attractive than demons. Who'd have thought, right?

"Welcome, ladies. Please sit." Barbara indicated three overstuffed leather chairs opposite her imposing solid wood desk. She retook her own seat and the smile dimmed. "I believe I know why you're here."

"Because you had a premonition?" I quipped, and she shook her head.

"I did, but not about you visiting. Robin called me." Barbara smiled.

This startled me for a moment. I hadn't realized they'd mended that particular fence. It was only a month or so ago that Robin was still Barbara's minion, and when Robin refused to kill her now-boyfriend, Jackson, Barbara tried to have Robin killed in retaliation. It was all very cloak-and-dagger, to be honest.

"You had a premonition?" Robin asked.

"Yes. Not about Catherine," she clarified. "About integration and protection of supernatural beings."

"What did you see?" Robin asked.

"It was typically vague, but showed the human and supernatural worlds as united. It also showed my role. I plan to introduce new legislation that will become the standard across this country for human-supernatural relations."

"That's fantastic," Catherine said.

"When are you introducing it?" I asked, my mind already wondering if I could get her on my show, or maybe even the evening news, to discuss this legislation.

Barbara chuckled. "Tomorrow night, and yes, Liz, I'd like some air time. If you can squeeze me in."

I grinned. "You know I can. I'll have my producer contact you. We're a little busy, as you know."

Barbara's smile slipped. "Yes, I'm aware of the deadline."

Anxiety whipped through me at the direct reminder of my looming death. I smiled wider to hide the discomfort. "We'll figure it out before that. I still have over 24 hours."

"Good luck. Let me know if I can do anything."

"We will—"

"Actually, Barbara," Catherine interrupted me. She stared down at her fidgeting hands for a moment. "I don't know how your ability works, but can you… direct… a premonition?"

Barbara's brow furrowed. "I'm not sure I understand. Do you mean control a premonition? No, I can't."

"Can you think about a topic to prompt a premonition?"

Barbara placed her hands on the desk top. She nodded, her fingernails tapping out a rhythm.

We remained quiet while she considered the question.

"I haven't directly tried before, but I've had times where a premonition followed thinking about a topic, so it's possible."

"I'd very much appreciate if you could try to find out something about me, my future."

Barbara nodded. "Let me give it a whirl." She closed her eyes, allowed her arms to lay loosely at her sides in the chair.

I tried to look at the others with my peripheral vision, afraid to move lest the spell be broken. Not a real spell, of course, the spell of wonderment. I felt a laugh bubble up and realized that my anxiety was increasing. What if we didn't like what she told us about Catherine's future? Worse, what if I ask her to do the same for me, and she sees nothing because I'm dead? My heart rate sped up at these thoughts. With supreme effort, I shut them off and focused on Barbara. I noted that her eyes moved rapidly beneath her closed lids, almost like she was dreaming. I hoped this meant that she was seeing something helpful. Barbara frowned and Catherine gasped. That couldn't be good.

Barbara's eyes snapped open. It was interesting to watch her orient herself to her current surroundings. The awareness increased until she smiled at us.

"That was amazing," she said.

"It worked?" Catherine asked.

"It did." Barbara inhaled deeply, perhaps arranging her thoughts. "I saw you, Catherine, and Rowan, the time-traveling ghost. You were both frowning. Fear and anger saturated the premonition. It was definitely not a happy meeting."

"What were they doing?" I asked.

"That's where it becomes vague. They were in a room together. Perhaps a ballroom? Some kind of larger space, it seemed. But, dark, as if there weren't any windows, and few lights had been turned on. They'd been arguing, I believe. Then the image became fuzzy. The best way to describe it is that mist swirled around."

"That's all," Catherine said, voice tinged with disappointment.

"Not quite. I thought the vision was complete and I was seeing it fade. But I don't think that's correct. It appeared that Catherine and Rowan were fading in and out, of existence or of our timeline. Which makes sense for the ghost, depleting her energy and all that." She frowned at Catherine. "It doesn't make sense for you."

I was already shaking my head at Barbara's conclusion. "That's already happened," I explained. "That happened yesterday."

"Not possible," Barbara countered. "I don't see the past, only the future."

"It's not possible that your powers have changed?" I challenged, and she tilted her head at me.

"It's not."

I suddenly felt like a tiny bug about to be squished. She'd maintained a few of her demon mannerisms.

"I don't understand," Catherine muttered.

"It's simple. It's going to happen again." Barbara shrugged at what to her was obvious.

Catherine paled. Robin patted her arm. "It's going to be okay."

"Thank you for the information, Barbara," I said. "This has been illuminating." Barbara chuckled at my formality. I stood and faced the others in the chairs. "It's time we revisit with Olivia and find out what else the archangel knows."

CHAPTER TWELVE

Catherine called Olivia, who agreed to meet us at Catherine's condo, only a few blocks from Barbara's office. Robin snagged a parking spot just outside the building. I glanced at the sky as we hurried across the street. Dark billowy clouds overhead threatened rain. I sniffed and decided it smelled like rain. Maybe we'd get a small squall. We entered the foyer and Catherine waved at the guard… doorman… security. I wasn't sure what she called him.

The elevator brought us to the 20th floor and Catherine led us down a short hallway to her door. "Does anybody want a drink?" Um, yes, we did. "Have a seat while I grab them."

Robin and I sat at the wooden dining table. I swiveled my head, taking in the space. Just a studio, but high ceilings and amazing floor-to-ceiling windows made it seem bigger. I loved my little house, but this wasn't too bad either.

Catherine set wine glasses in front of us. "All I have is white right now. Hope that's okay."

I lifted my glass. "A toast. To figuring out Catherine's importance and keeping me alive." Our glasses clinked. A knock sounded. "Perfect timing. That must be Olivia."

Catherine hopped up and went to the door to let Olivia in. Catherine grabbed a glass of wine for the archangel on the way back to the table.

"Thank you for agreeing to meet with us," I started. "Random question first. How come you didn't just materialize in here?"

Olivia laughed and shook her head. "That would be rude. This is a private home and nobody is in danger."

"Not at the moment, anyway," I quipped.

"What can I do for you ladies?" Olivia asked.

All eyes turned to Catherine who toyed with a cuticle. If she kept that up, she'd be a bloody mess. She chugged a large swallow of wine before answering. "We've met with the Witches Council and Mayor Barbara Knollman to gather more information. We've confirmed some of what you told us. There's something different enough about me to mess with the magical energy of the city." Catherine chugged another swallow of wine. "I'm going to have another run-in with Rowan, and neither of us will be happy about it." She looked at me and Robin. "But we aren't getting any details." Frustration saturated her voice. "We aren't getting anything we can take action on."

"So, you decided to try me again?"

"Yes," Catherine said.

"I've already told you everything that I can," Olivia reminded us.

"That's not good enough," Catherine snapped, and my wide eyes met Robin's. I didn't think I'd ever heard Catherine get angry before.

Olivia's eyes darkened for a moment, then they cleared and she smiled. "I'm afraid it is what it is."

"More riddles." Catherine's hand tightened around the stem of her wine glass. Robin reached to place her hand over Catherine's.

"Everyone is doing the best they can," she assured the upset empath.

"Are they though?" I asked. Catherine had a point. I stared at the archangel. "Please give a straight answer. Do you know something you're not sharing? Or are you really in the dark as much as we are?"

Olivia reflected my stare. She didn't answer.

My brief show of nerves faltered with her continued silence. She couldn't send me to hell for being difficult. Could she?

Olivia's expression softened. "I like you, Liz."

"Thanks?"

"You never hesitate to say what you're thinking."

I shrugged, ears burning with the compliment. Or at least, I assumed it was a compliment.

"I wouldn't say I'm as in the dark as the three of you, no. Neither would I say that I know exactly what's going to happen. Timelines can be tricky. It's not always clear what will happen in one versus another."

My head throbbed. I held up a hand to stop her. "Are we a primary timeline?"

Olivia chuckled. "For you, you are."

"Riddles again," Robin sighed.

"Ladies. I'm not trying to be difficult. It's as I said before. Based on what I can see, you are on the right track."

"How is this a track? We don't know where we're going," Catherine spat out.

Olivia turned her speculative gaze on me again and I squirmed. "Interesting."

"What?" I asked.

"You're about to get a very clear direction."

"What does that mean?" I asked uneasily. "The last time we got a clear direction, Rowan attacked us." My eyebrows shot up. "That's it, isn't it? Rowan's going to attack us again." Robin gasped. Catherine chugged more wine.

Olivia shook her head. "That I cannot answer."

"I'm right," I crowed. "I know I am." I sobered. "Although I don't know why I'm happy about that. Last time, she nearly turned us into barbecue," I groused.

Olivia laughed. "That is all I have for you. Good luck."

Our responses were said into the void as Olivia winked out of Catherine's dining area.

"That was fun," Catherine mumbled.

"No, this is good," I disagreed excitedly. "We just have to be ready."

"I think we need to make sure the two of you aren't ever alone," Robin said.

Catherine and I exchanged glances. We nodded our acceptance.

"I'll stay with Catherine for tonight," Robin said, "after we bring Liz to her date with Tony." She grinned.

Mention of my date released tension in the room, for everybody except me. I responded with a tight smile. Was I making a mistake? The journalist in me said no, because I'd find out about another supernatural being. The woman in me… I decided not to think about that just yet.

"What happened to supernatural-beings-and-humans-can't-have-a-future?" Catherine teased.

"Have you decided whether to accept Alex's proposal?" I responded with a wink.

Robin snorted. Catherine reddened.

"Okay, this has passed the point of usefulness," Robin concluded, though with a smile. "Liz, are you ready to see Tony?"

I stood with a sharp nod. "Yes, I am. Let's go."

My mind swam as we took the elevator to the foyer. Kaleidoscope emotions filled me. Excitement. Dread. Elation. Trepidation. Desire. My heart hammered in my chest. I might have had mixed emotions about humans and supernaturals, but one stood out above the others. Longing. The intensity surprised me, but the thought of Tony's protective nature, sweet personality, and, of course, hotness brought out such a sense of longing. I could only hope the evening lived up to my internal hype.

CHAPTER THIRTEEN

Tony stood outside Fleming's, looking suave, but uncomfortable, his broad shoulders trapped in a dark, pin-striped suit, no tie. We'd had enough time, and Robin and Catherine had been willing, to swing by my not-exactly-on-the-way house so I could change. Now I was glad I did. Robin pulled her car alongside the front and I opened the door.

"Looking good, Tony," she called out to him. He smiled, though his eyes quickly found mine.

"Thanks, Robin, Catherine. I'll see you later." I closed the door on their quiet chuckling.

"You look wonderful." I walked to his side, looked up into his brown eyes. The heat between us was obvious.

"You're beautiful," he responded, his gaze drinking in my fitted, knee-length, purple dress showcasing my curves. "Are you hungry?"

"Oh, yes," I breathed out.

Tony waggled his eyebrows at me and I laughed, breaking the sensual tension. "Let's go in, then," he said. He held the door open so I could enter.

After giving his name to the hostess, we followed the young woman in a black cocktail dress to a booth on the opposite side of the dimly lit restaurant. We slid onto the red vinyl, maybe leather, seats around the table. Dinnerware and cutlery, including a rather large steak knife, sat atop the crisp white tablecloth. The hostess assured us our waitress would be right over.

Heat radiated off of Tony. I didn't think it was just attraction. He seemed to run hot. As in, a high temperature. My silly thoughts led me to giggle.

"What has you so entertained?"

Let's get to it. "You. I was thinking that your body temperature sits higher than most."

"Interesting observation," he responded. "Why do you suppose that might be?"

I pondered the question. "Because of whatever being you are?"

He nodded. "Have you guessed what being yet?"

"Nope. I've thought about your intensity, your size, your hearing. Your smell." I inhaled deeply, enjoying the earthy scent of him. "Your scent." His eyes dilated and I fidgeted.

"That doesn't suggest anything specific?" he teased.

A thought niggled my brain but left before I could grab it. I shook my head.

"What do you smell?"

"Floral, unspecified, though. Earthy, like after a rain."

He tilted his head.

"What?"

"Most people can't smell what you're smelling."

"Why do you suppose I can?"

"I don't know," he said slowly. "But, a deal's a deal. You met me for dinner, so I'll tell you what I am. Though I hadn't thought we'd jump right in with it," he admitted.

I laughed. "I'm a journalist for a reason. I want to know everything, and I don't wait very well." Tony joined my laughter for a moment. He broke eye contact and reached for his water glass. His hand trembled. "Are you nervous?" I asked softly.

He drank half the glass in a large gulp. Set the glass back down and smoothed out nonexistent wrinkles in the tablecloth. "I am," he said. His eyes met mine. The naked fear there shocked me. "I haven't gone on a date in a long time. But, there's something about you."

"There is?"

"You're intelligent, beautiful, tenacious, stubborn."

"Those last aren't always considered positives."

"I don't want an easy, passive woman by my side."

"If you want a challenge, I'm sure I'm up for that," I quipped.

"I don't want to scare you off. Especially knowing your concerns…"

"We can take it one day at a time." And I meant it. "What are you?"

"I'm a shifter."

That took a second to process. "A werewolf?"

Tony belly laughed, drawing the eyes of couples at nearby tables. He held up a hand in apology, leaned in closer to me. "Not every shifter is a wolf. Try another animal."

My brain couldn't think of another animal. But a shifter made perfect sense with what I'd seen so far. A realization hit. "That's how you could hear me at your café."

"I told you I have excellent hearing."

He waited for me to figure it out. "Tell me what you are," I begged.

"I'm a were-panther."

My eyes widened. "That's so cool." I reached out to cover his hand with my own, enjoying the body heat combined with the heat of attraction. "Is that what I smell? A sleek black kitty."

"Panther," he corrected with a wink.

"I'd love to see that one day," slipped out, and he tensed.

"Maybe one day," he allowed.

Discrete coughing drew our attention; the waitress had arrived. Tony ordered for both of us – steak well done for me, run-it-through-a-warm-room for him. I wrinkled my nose at his choice and he gave me a one-shoulder shrug.

"It tastes better to me."

The waitress left.

"Where are you from?"

"Italy."

"You have such a slight accent. I couldn't place it."

"I've been in the US for some time."

Nerves fluttered. "How long?"

Tony chuckled. "Don't worry. I'm not as old as some of your friends."

"Some of them are hundreds of years old." My mind still had trouble processing that. I wasn't even thirty yet. I couldn't imagine Mia's over 200 years. Or Barbara's 400, I think it was, maybe 500 years.

"I'm not in the plurals yet," he said.

My eyebrows rose. "100 years old?"

"Thereabouts."

I shook my head. "It's seriously not fair how you supernaturals get to live forever but still look so darn young."

"I won't live forever. Shifters aren't immortal."

"I guess that's a good thing," I responded with a nervous chuckle. "However, I'll still grow old while you continue to look like this." I waved my hand up and down. There was a teasing quality to my comment, but Tony didn't miss the harsh truth underneath.

"It's no different than some of your other friends' relationships: Catherine and Alex, Evie and Ryan, Mia and Jacob. It's like one of them said. All relationships have challenges. This would just be one specific to a human-supernatural relationship."

At his repeated use of the word relationship, I grew more certain that I wanted that with him. His eyes dilated again, and he placed his other hand on mine so it was sandwiched between his.

"How do you do that?" I asked.

"Do what?"

"Seem to know what I'm thinking?"

"I don't. Know what you're thinking."

"Yet, your responses suggest you do," I countered.

He gave a lazy smile. "Your body tells me what you're thinking."

My body? A flush crept up my neck.

"Like right now."

"What do you see?" I whispered.

He shook his head, eyes holding mine. "Your physical reactions are easy for me to sense. I can hear everything from the tiniest change in your breath to the racing of your heart. Smell the release of hormones."

I pulled my hand from his and sat back. "You can smell me?"

He looked perplexed. "How is that any different from when you said you liked my scent?"

Another nervous chuckle bubbled to the surface. "Oh, right. That makes sense." I gave a shy smile. "I think I understand more now. Tell me about Italy."

"Those pictures in my café?"

"Yes?"

"I took those as a teenaged shifter sixty years ago."

My mouth dropped open and I snapped it shut. "Tell me everything."

And he did. Tony regaled me with stories of his youth in Italy, his parents' decision to move to America, their decision ten years ago to return to Italy. When our steaks arrived, we paused long enough to scarf the delectable food. Soon the restaurant was closing and it was time to leave.

Tony stood, offered a hand to assist me out of the booth. His warm skin caressed mine with just this bare touch. We held hands traversing the restaurant, releasing only when he held the door open again for us to leave.

I suddenly laughed and he looked at me askance. "I just realized that Robin gave me a ride here, so I need to call her for a ride back."

"You know I can give you a ride."

"I know." I felt like a nervous teenager after a first date. Would he kiss me, should I let him? But, with a grown-up twist. Would I, should I, invite him in? Except I was staying at Catherine's tonight, so that wasn't even an option. Confusing disappointment flooded through me.

Tony stepped closer, used a finger to lift my chin. "Liz, relax. We can go as slow as you want. You don't have to invite me in." His eyes danced with merriment and I shook my head.

"That'll take some getting used to," I muttered. A smile broke across my face. "But, thank you. I knew you were a gentleman. And I like you, so…"

Tony leaned down.

My lips parted to accept his kiss—

"Time's running out," a harsh voice interrupted.

Tony and I sprang apart before our lips touched. My brain, already getting a workout this evening, had trouble comprehending what I saw. "Rowan?"

"Elizabeth. I told you what would happen if you didn't stop investigating. Yet, you spent all day doing exactly that."

To my surprise, the ghost sounded exasperated by me. Well, she wasn't the first and she wouldn't be the last.

"I'm on a date, Rowan," I pointed out, like I could reason with her.

"I'm aware of that." Her blue eyes darkened. "Since concern for yourself or my future family didn't seem to make a dent, I'm trying a new approach."

Fear shot through me. "What do you mean?"

Rowan dematerialized and then rematerialized, next to Tony. We turned to her in surprise. Rowan wrapped her arms around Tony, who growled. Just like a panther would.

Tony's skin rolled, the bones moving beneath. As if they were trying to reshape themselves. His brown eyes flashed an impossible shade of green. Hair sprouted then retracted along his limbs, his face. He growled again, his body becoming almost liquid with the changes he was trying to force. I realized he was trying to shift just as Rowan shot me a triumphant glare. The two became translucent and vanished.

"Tony!" I screamed into the dark night.

CHAPTER FOURTEEN

Tony was gone. Rowan had taken him. These thoughts swirled like a maelstrom in my mind. What was I supposed to do? The sound of a door opening drew my attention. I turned back toward the restaurant. A middle-aged man with a trim beard stood there, mouth agape.

"Are you okay, ma'am? Did I just see… what I thought I saw?"

I blinked, focused on the man. "If you just saw a ghost kidnap my date, then yes. Yes, you did."

If it was possible for the man's mouth to fall open even more, it did with my explanation. "Do you need help?" He asked the question, but the terror in his eyes made it clear he wouldn't know what to do if I said yes.

"No, thank you." I approached him, slowing when he tensed. "There's nothing you can do," I assured him. "Go back inside. I know who to call."

Nodding his head like he had a broken neck, the man retreated into the restaurant. "Good luck," floated past me as the door closed. The lock turned.

I pulled my cellphone from my purse and autodialed Catherine.

"Hey Liz, I'm surprised to hear from you," her voice answered. "Figured you'd get a ride here from Tony." I heard Robin's laughter in the background.

I couldn't find my voice.

"Liz?" Catherine's tone sharpened. "Are you there? Is everything okay?"

I shook my head before remembering she couldn't see me. "No," I whispered. "Tony's gone. Rowan took him."

"What? Did you just say Rowan has Tony?"

"She showed up at the end of dinner. Yelled at me for continuing the investigation. And took Tony because she knows I like him." I explained how Rowan materialized and dematerialized.

Catherine and Robin held a mumbled conversation. "We'll be there in fifteen minutes."

The call ended, leaving me alone with my thoughts. If I hadn't accepted the date with Tony, he wouldn't have been kidnapped. I was cool with risking my own life, not someone else's. Although Rowan had pointed out that I ignored her plea to save her family. My heartbeat thundered through my body. Was she right? Did I only care now that someone I had feelings for had been taken?

No, that wasn't accurate. Rowan's tale of the future may or may not be accurate. And, Olivia insisted that I stay on this path. I was right to keep investigating Catherine. I had to be. But if Tony was hurt because of it—

Stop! This wasn't helping me or Tony. I needed to think. Where could Rowan have taken him? Barbara's premonition showed Catherine and Rowan in a cavernous, windowless room. Could that be where Tony was? Or was that a separate future incident?

Frustration thrummed through me. I tapped my foot on the concrete. The cool wind blew across my skin, lifting my short curls away from my face. My eyes closed. I heard tires on pavement and then a horn. I opened my eyes to see Robin's Jetta.

"Do you think she took Tony to where Barbara saw Catherine and Rowan's showdown?" I greeted the women upon entering the backseat of the car.

Robin pulled away from the restaurant. "I don't know. That's a good question. Could give us a place to start investigating."

"Can you guys think of a large space without windows, though?" Catherine asked, the tip of her right index finger tapping her chin while she thought.

"Most theaters would fit the bill," I said. "Or maybe larger business meeting rooms at some of the casinos. Or even rooms at the convention center." My voice had taken on a gloomy tone with so many options.

"Oof, yeah, there are lots of possibilities," Robin responded. "How would we even go about investigating them?"

"And do we have the time for that?" Catherine asked.

"We have no idea. Bottom line is we don't know Rowan's timeline," I said, sharper than I intended. "Sorry. Frustrated. It would have been nice for Rowan to give us a clue."

"Why would she?" Robin asked.

"What do you mean?" Catherine asked.

Robin slowed the car to a stop at a red light and turned in her seat to look between Catherine and me. "Why do you think she abducted Tony?"

"To force us to look for him, I assume." I lifted my hands in question.

"But, why?" Robin asked again, facing forward to watch the road. The car shifted when the light changed to green.

A lightbulb went off. "Oh, I get it."

"What am I missing?" Catherine asked.

"Rowan likely has no real intention of hurting Tony. She's trying to stop my investigation into you, Catherine."

Robin nodded. She slid the car into a street parking spot across from Catherine's building. I gathered my purse to exit the vehicle.

Outside in the wind, I raised my voice to be heard. "My guess is that she hopes to distract us from investigating long enough for the timeline to change in her favor."

The three of us hurried across the street to the building. Catherine waved at the security guy behind the desk and we continued to the elevator past the mailroom.

"How will she know the timeline has changed?" Catherine questioned.

I frowned. "I don't know. Based on movies like *Bill & Ted's Excellent Adventure*, any changes in the timeline automatically take effect simultaneously across the entire timeline. So maybe she somehow will know." Uncertainty tinged my voice but Catherine and Robin were smiling.

The elevator pinged at the 20th floor.

"I love that that's your reference for time travel knowledge," Catherine said with a chuckle.

"It's all I have," I responded with a wry smile.

Robin and I followed Catherine into her studio loft. "Drinks?" she asked.

"Definitely," I responded, heading for the maroon couch facing the floor-to-ceiling windows. At night, the view from here of Fremont and the Arts District was cool. I sat, crossed my legs, wished I had pants, remembered I had some in my bag in the other room, decided I didn't care enough to get up to change.

Catherine placed three glasses of white wine on the coffee table, then she and Robin sat on either side of me. We reached for the glasses at the same time, eliciting chuckles.

"What do we think?" Catherine asked.

"Our theory is that this is purely a tactic," Robin summarized. "Rowan won't hurt Tony. She's just holding him to stop you until the timeline changes sufficiently for her to know she's saved herself and her family."

"But, if she saves herself in the future, she won't have to come back to the past," Catherine mused. "Would she just vanish?"

The three of us swallowed large gulps of wine.

"Time travel is by far too complicated," I said.

"Rather than getting stuck on the semantics, or physics, or whatever," Robin continued, "let's figure out what we're going to do."

"Great," Catherine agreed. "What are we going to do?"

We burst into laughter, that innocent but huge question somehow breaking the tension that had been building since I placed my call to Catherine.

"Oh my," I blurted out, then stopped. The ladies waited, but I wasn't sure if I should say the next part. I hesitated.

"What is it, Liz?" Catherine asked.

"Are you guys aware of Tony, what he is?" I asked.

"Yes," Robin answered, though Catherine appeared confused. "I assume he told you." Robin directed this at me and when I nodded, she turned to Catherine. "He's a shifter, a were-panther."

Catherine drank another gulp of wine. "Cool," she mumbled around the liquid.

"He started to shift when she grabbed him. He was still shifting when they dematerialized."

Robin and Catherine stared at me. "Hmm," Robin said, though declined to elaborate.

"What?" Catherine asked. Understanding dawned as the realization hit.

"Is Rowan guarding a panther, a human, or a half-shifted were-panther?" I asked what we were now all thinking.

Catherine raised her eyes to the ceiling. We waited. She looked back at us. "Does it matter? I don't think it does. He's a powerful being. He'd want us to do what we needed to do."

"You're right," I agreed. "And what we need to do is show Rowan that she can't force us to do things her way."

"What do you have in mind?" Robin asked.

In answer, I jumped from the couch and headed for the dining area table where I'd dropped my purse. I fumbled for my cellphone and pulled it out. I scrolled for a specific number. Catherine and Robin had followed, now stood next to me.

"Who are you calling?" Robin asked.

"Your favorite person," I joked. Her brow furrowed while she tried to think who I meant.

"It's kind of late for a social call," the voice on the other end said, but without rancor.

"Good evening, Barbara," I said.

Robin rolled her eyes. "Barbara and I are good now," she whispered.

"Sorry for the late call." I met Catherine's and Robin's eyes with a grin. "Any chance you'd be up for a last-minute interview tomorrow morning? We need your help."

CHAPTER FIFTEEN

"Good morning in the Valley," I greeted my viewers per usual. "Today we have a special report and will be delaying our original story about local author Brian Bunter's new book until later in the week. Instead, Mayor Barbara Knollman will be in the studio to discuss her exciting new proposed law. After the break." Sweat broke out despite my antiperspirant. I didn't get nervous doing my show, so I knew the real cause. Today's interview. I turned to my subject, sitting with no visible discomfort or anxiety in the stuffed blue chair next to mine.

"You seem amazingly calm," I said.

Barbara smiled. "I have nothing to be nervous about, Liz. This is the right path."

I harrumphed. "Must be nice to be an angel with precognition."

She laughed.

"Back in five," a voice came from my ear bud. I faced the nearest camera and readied my smile – and steadied my nerves.

"Before I turn the interview over to the mayor, a quick recap for viewers who may have missed yesterday's show. Two days ago, a time traveling ghost from the future arrived to tell me I would die in three days. She demanded I cease my investigations into a certain supernatural being here in town and cease my support of Mayor Knollman's initiatives. Spoiler alert, I didn't." I winked at the camera before adopting a serious countenance.

"Today is Day 3. If this ghost is correct, today is the day of my death." I ignored gasps I heard in the studio. Not helpful. "But you guys know me. You've been watching me for years now. It's not in my nature to quit. Plus, this is bigger than one person." I faced Barbara.

"You and I are on the same page here," I said. "We understand there are humans and other beings who want to stop progress, for whatever reasons."

"Yes, we do understand. And they are wrong."

"To the point as always, Mayor." I chuckled and gestured toward her nearest camera. "The floor is yours. What is your proposal?"

Barbara smiled into the camera. "Good morning. Today has the potential to be historic. This afternoon I will propose new legislation that will be the first step toward allowing supernatural beings, such as myself," she reminded viewers, "to fully integrate into society. Meaning, we won't have to hide." She frowned. "Now, I can hear – well, not literally, that's not my supernatural skill – the objections of some of you." She tilted her head. "What are the dangers? What are the protections for humanity? These are legitimate concerns," she conceded.

"Let's look at it another way. We have always existed. We have always lived among you. What my legislation will allow is for us to do so in full view. To ensure all are protected, my proposal includes creating a Working Group to research and make recommendations for managing expectations between humans and supernaturals. Part of that will involve developing a direct working relationship between the paranormal underworld governing body and the city council. Since I am the head of both organizations, I imagine this will be fairly painless."

Barbara glanced at me. "Did you have any questions, Liz?"

"How will appointment to the supernatural governing body work? Will there be voting? Will humans be able to vote for supernatural representatives?"

"Those are all excellent questions. The purpose of the Working Group will be to answer them. That may not be a satisfactory answer right now, but this is the best way forward. I am not a supreme leader," she said with a chuckle. "Nor am I going to demand certain treatment for those of my kind. The Working Group will have representatives from multiple constituency and supernatural groups, appointed from within each and without interference from the others. This will allow for a diversity of opinions and suggestions for the best ways to move forward with integration.

"These are exciting times. Las Vegas has an unprecedented opportunity to be on the front lines of progress." She turned back toward me. "Thank you, Liz, for this opportunity to address the city."

I nodded and turned to the camera. "You heard it here first, folks. Las Vegas will blaze the trail in human-supernatural relations. Tune in tonight when we'll give you the results of this historic vote."

The producer counted us off the air in my ear. I faced Barbara again. "Thank you again for coming on. I know it was for your benefit too, but it's time to bring this to a head. Without me losing my head."

Barbara's brow furrowed. "I hope it didn't put you in too much danger."

"I was already in danger," I responded with a shrug. "Now we see if taunting the ghost worked."

CHAPTER SIXTEEN

Taunting Rowan had been a calculated risk on our parts. Catherine, Robin, and I figured that the ghost would see what I was doing and identify that we were deliberately taunting her. We hoped she would refrain from coming after me or harming Tony because she would assume that would play into our hands somehow if she did. But, a side effect of her unreleased anger might be a buildup of her own energy. And that, our biggest hope, would be something we could track and home in on.

Thus, we found ourselves back on Industrial Road visiting the Witches Council. Catherine, Robin, and I sat facing the five witches on the council.

A space had been made between us and them, bigger than before. I'd called Jessica prior to my show, and she'd promised to have everyone assembled in time. She'd delivered.

"Welcome," Jessica said. "I've brought the other councilmembers up to speed with the plan and we're ready to go."

"It was quite ingenious," Theresa added. "I could sense the magical energy change as the show went on."

"We should be able to pinpoint the highest concentration of that energy in the city," Matt assured us, running his hand over his bald head.

The witches stood and we scrambled to follow suit.

"You'll notice we've already pulled chairs out of the way to allow room to create the circle," Jessica explained. She approached us, carrying a bag, presumably of supplies for whatever spell we were about to cast.

"We'll conduct a finding ritual," Theresa said, reaching into the bag to pull out four candles. She spoke as she placed and lit each candle in the corners of the space. "These are to help cleanse the energy and call the corners for the ritual." She glanced around at the assembled people. "We have more than enough witches to channel the elements for the ritual, so we'll use those of us with the stronger relevant magic. Given my sensing abilities, I'll take point." She seemed to direct this explanation more at us than her fellow councilmembers, but they nodded when she finished.

Theresa placed and lit a red candle. "Robin, I know you're not a member of the council, but since you're able to control energy, including lightning, you will pull the energy of fire." Robin stood next to the candle and closed her eyes. She murmured under her breath.

I already knew how Robin had summoned and directed a bolt of lightning to kill the witch that Barbara had sent to kill Robin's boyfriend last month. An involuntary shiver went through me at the thought of that much power. And, yet, Catherine was the one who was impacting the timeline. I refocused on the scene before me.

Theresa placed and lit a blue candle. "Marcie, with your feminine energy and emotion skills, you will channel water energy." The young blond stood beside her candle, closed her eyes, and joined Robin in softly chanting.

Hmm, what could 'emotion skills' be? Catherine could sense others' emotions and Mia could manipulate others' emotions. At which end of that spectrum did Marcie's abilities reside? She looked so young and innocent to possess a skill like that.

Theresa placed and lit a white candle. "Jessica, with your purity of spirit, you will channel the energy of the air." The redhead took her place beside the candle and joined in the quiet chanting.

Purity of spirit perplexed me. Weren't they all what were known as white witches? Wouldn't they all have pure spirits? This whole process fascinated me.

Theresa placed and lit a green candle. "And I will channel the energy of the earth herself. This will allow me to narrow my focus on the sensed energy to a specific location on the planet – ideally, where Rowan has taken our friend."

Catherine and I, along with the other members of the council not involved in the ritual, remained outside the invisible circle watching. The chanting stayed indecipherable and then stopped. Theresa's eyes opened.

"Thank you, goddess, for your support of our circle. Thank you to each of the elements. We focus our intent on finding our lost friend. Show me the location of the energy spike from this morning."

Unlike the earlier rhythmic quality, Theresa's request was surprisingly matter-of-fact, almost conversational. My gaze wandered across the faces of the others in the circle. Their eyes remained closed, though they stayed quiet.

Theresa's eyes widened for a moment and then closed again. I saw movement under her eyelids like she was dreaming. Was she having a vision? This was so cool.

In concert, all four women's heads dropped, chins resting on chests. A simultaneous deep inhale, exhale, and their eyes opened. Smiles blossomed across their faces, mirrored by the other members of the council not taking part in the circle. Catherine and I exchanged a confused glance. Did it work?

"It worked," Theresa explained to us, as though reading my mind.

"Where is he?" I asked. Please be in town. In our own time. Unharmed.

The four women blew out their candles before Theresa answered. "He's okay, in our time, and still in Las Vegas."

"Thank goodness," I said with a palpable sense of relief.

"He's downtown," she continued.

"The Strip, Arts District, or some other downtown." I ticked off the possibilities on my fingers.

Theresa smiled. "He seems to be in a wedding chapel in the Arts District."

"That'll be perfect for you, Catherine. You should call Alex," I quipped, and she paled, shooting me a not-very-nice look. What can I say, I crack jokes when I'm nervous.

"There are a lot of wedding chapels in the Arts District," Robin pointed out. "Any chance you could narrow that down?"

"Yes. Other than a small altar for the vows, the room was nondescript, so my best guess is a chapel that is currently closed," Theresa said.

"Could be one that's defunct," Jessica offered.

"Or one that's undergoing renovations," Catherine mused.

"It also sounds like one that's not theme-based," I said. "Anything else that could help us eliminate?" The thought of calling hundreds of chapels made my stomach hurt.

Theresa shook her head. "No, unfortunately."

Tension in the room spiked with this statement.

"I have an idea," Catherine said, blue eyes sparkling. "I forget the full name, but there's a wedding association group here in town. If a chapel is closed for renovations or has recently shut down entirely, they most likely would know about it. We just need to call and ask them."

"That's brilliant, Catherine." I pulled out my phone to google for association names. "Which one of these is it?" There were several listed in Las Vegas and Clark County.

Catherine frowned. Her eyes scanned the listings. "That's it," she said, pointing at my phone. She snatched it from my hand and pressed the hyperlink. "I've got this," she said, walking toward the far corner of the room for quiet and privacy.

"Okay, then." I faced the others. "What's our plan once Catherine figures out which chapel it is? We're not going in there, guns blazing."

"This is the wild west," Robin said with a grin.

"Not that wild," I countered with a chuckle, then sobered. "We don't know what condition Tony will be in when we arrive, so we need to plan for no assistance from him." The others nodded. "Theresa, since you sense energy, would you mind coming with us?"

"Of course."

"Robin, we may need your summoning power," I warned.

"I'm ready."

"Marcie, with your 'emotion skills'—" I arched an eyebrow at her. "—it may be necessary to reason with Rowan."

Marcie gave me an enigmatic grin and nodded.

"I, unfortunately, am a useless human," I half-joked, "but my focus will be on getting Tony."

"No doubt," Catherine ribbed me as she rejoined the group. "We know you want to get him."

I rolled my eyes at her. "And?"

"I've narrowed it to three possibilities, all within a few blocks of each other, centered near Bonneville."

"Robin, you'll drive. Catherine, Marcie, Theresa, and I will go with. The rest of you stay here on standby, in case we need anything," I directed.

"Sounds good, General Addison," Robin teased me.

"Neither Tony nor I are dying today. I don't care what Rowan the time-traveling ghost has planned." The hairs on my arm rose with the tension in the room. "Let's go."

CHAPTER SEVENTEEN

The drive to Bonneville Avenue from Industrial Road was under ten minutes. With only three places to check, I hoped we'd locate Tony and Rowan in under an hour. "You know, if this was a movie, it'd be the last place we look," I joked. "To heighten the tension."

The others laughed. "Maybe we should start with the one we'd check last, try to subvert that ending," Theresa suggested with a smile.

"Too twisty for me – we'll stick with going in order from closest to farthest," Robin said. "After all, I'm driving."

"I've decided to say yes to Alex," Catherine blurted out.

Theresa and Marcie appeared confused, but Robin and I whooped in pleasure and expressed our congratulations.

"My boyfriend proposed," Catherine explained to the councilmembers. They added their congratulations.

"What tipped the decision?" I asked.

"I thought about everything we've been through, how nothing is certain, and when you're in love… you shouldn't let it go or live in fear."

An image of Tony's grinning face flashed in my mind. "Yeah, that makes sense." I felt Robin's eyes on me. "Yes?"

"Does this change anything for you?" She smirked.

I twisted in the front seat to look at Theresa and Marcie in the back with Catherine. "Previously, I've expressed that I didn't think humans and supernaturals could have a future," I explained to them. "I may have been mistaken." I ran a hand through my hair. "To say I'm feeling ambivalent would be an understatement."

"How did your date with Tony go?" Robin asked. "I mean, before Rowan kidnapped him," she amended.

A flush crept across my face. "Really well. I like him. We're going to go out again."

"That's wonderful," Catherine said. The others murmured their agreement.

"That's why I can't die today, and neither can Tony," I stated.

"We're at the first chapel," Robin announced. She pulled over to the side of the road.

Everyone faced the small white building. Even from the car, we could see a sign posted on the pink door. It likely said closed for renovations.

I shook my head. "I doubt this is it. Too small, I think. Didn't Barbara say the room was large, cavernous even?"

"She did," Robin agreed. "But premonitions aren't an exact science," she reminded me.

"Do you sense her energy?" I asked Theresa.

"I don't."

"Are you sure?" Catherine asked.

"She's not here."

"On we go to option number two," Robin declared and eased the car back onto the road. She drove up the street a few blocks. Before she'd even parked, Theresa was nodding her head.

"I sense Rowan," she said. "If Tony's with her, he's here."

Catherine poked me in the shoulder. "Looks like it's not going to be the last place we check."

"Guess we're not that interesting of a movie," I quipped.

Everyone laughed, dispelling the apprehension in the car. We stared at the building. It was a two-story house, painted white with red accents. Pretty. Looked like a nice place to get married. I opened my car door, prompting the others to do the same.

The five of us stood in front of the car, surveying the house further.

"Still not cavernous," I commented.

"Not an exact science," Robin repeated.

I smiled. "Let's go get my mate."

Mate? The word slipped out. I strode forward before anyone could comment. The sound of shoes scuffing on the concrete followed me from the street up to the door.

"They're definitely in there," Theresa whispered.

"Time for boldness," I said with false bravado and tried the door. It was unlocked and swung open to reveal a dark, dusty interior. "Here we go."

CHAPTER EIGHTEEN

The five of us crowded together in the foyer, listening for sounds in the converted home. Silence. Someone cleared their throat.

"Should we split up?" Catherine whispered.

I swiveled my head to take in the wooden stairs leading to who-knew-what upstairs, the two rooms on either side of the foyer, and a dark hallway leading to the back half of the home.

"That would make it faster," I began, "but, that always spells doom in the movies."

"Keeping with the movie theme, I see," Robin teased.

"We'll stick together," Catherine said.

Murmured agreement met the statement. I felt eyes on me and took charge. "We'll check the room on the left first." I strode in that direction, a quick walk of maybe five feet.

Our group stopped in the doorway. A basic chapel, with rows of folding chairs and a small raised altar, greeted us. Empty. We saw no places to hide, for either a manifested ghost or a shifted were-panther. They weren't here.

We backed into the foyer. I glanced up at the stairs. Would she have tried to take him up there? She wouldn't have to physically maneuver him. The ability to materialize and dematerialize made that a moot concern. I wondered whether to check from the back of the house, searching clockwise to end with the room on our right, or move from front to back, which would make the room on the right our next location.

Theresa spoke as I stepped toward the room on our right. "Rowan's energy is rising. She knows we're coming," she whispered.

My anxiety spiked, sending butterflies in motion in my belly and the blood coursing in my veins to thunder. The moment of truth. "Be ready." Marcie shifted to stand next to me, Robin behind her, with Catherine and Theresa bringing up the rear.

I flung the door open, like ripping off a band-aid. My feet carried me forward without thought and the others spread out beside me. We stood in our row of five, taking in the scene before us. We'd found Rowan and Tony.

Rowan stood at the altar, as though waiting for her bridegroom in her utilitarian jumpsuit. Pain sliced through me when I remembered that in her time, her husband and children were dead. Her red hair was like a fiery halo and her blue eyes flashed. Tony lay on the floor before her, in his panther form. He was magnificent, sleek black, eyes closed. Red glowing strands of energy wrapped around him.

"What are those?" I whispered, though Rowan's smirk told me she heard me too.

"I don't know," Theresa answered. "They're throwing off significant energy, with the same vibration of the ghost." Rowan's smirk slipped slightly, suggesting Theresa was correct in her analysis. Tony became translucent and then solidified again.

"Did you see that?" I squeaked out. "What's happening to him? Tony," I called out. He opened his eyes, seeing us for the first time. But not really. I saw no awareness. "Tony?" I whispered. He phased in and out again.

"Those are strands of time energy," Catherine suddenly said.

"They're what?" I asked, cutting my eyes to hers.

Wide eyed, she shook her head. "I have no idea. It just came into my head."

"I think I can control them," Robin said, under her breath.

Rowan's smile fell completely. "Enough."

All eyes returned to her.

"I know you held that broadcast to get at me," she said. "And I knew you would come."

"We're here now. What's next?" I asked. To my surprise, Rowan appeared near tears.

"None of this is what I wanted. I don't want anybody else to get hurt. I just want my family back," she whispered.

"Let Tony go," Marcie stepped forward and urged her. "Come with us to talk to the archangel. She can reassure you that your future isn't set in stone."

Rowan wavered. Marcie took another step forward. "I... no... I," Rowan stuttered, her eyes locked on Marcie's. "Stop! He's mine. I need to delay you longer. The timeline must change." Rowan's voice became frantic. She took several halting steps toward Marcie and Theresa, who had stepped to the left away from me, Catherine, and Robin.

"Her energy is depleting," Theresa said, voice barely above a whisper.

The rest of us were bewildered until it hit me. "Marcie's convinced her we're already rescuing Tony," I said in awe. Gasps met my explanation. Oh, but that meant we needed to actually rescue him now.

With a nudge to Robin's arm, I nodded in Tony's direction. He continued to phase in and out. "Now," I whispered. "While Marcie has Rowan... distracted." Robin and I raced to Tony's prone form. His eyes met mine; I swore he recognized me this time. Energy surged through me. I nodded at Robin, who placed her hands above Tony and closed her eyes. Her fingertips began to glow. We watched in fascination as the red energy bands surrounding Tony flowed up into Robin's hands. When the last wisp entered, Robin directed her fingertips toward the ground and the energy flowed below and dissipated. Panting, Robin turned to us.

"I've grounded the energy. We can grab him."

Tony stood on all four paws, blinking rapidly at us, trying to get his bearings. Robin appeared correct. The crackling energy bands were gone. I stepped toward him, grasped his snout between my hands and kissed his nose. Our eyes met and I chuckled. "You didn't think you'd get out of our second date that easily, did you?"

Tony's eyes danced in merriment and he chuffed at me, then licked my cheek. His tongue felt rough against my skin, yet sent a thrill through my body.

"Time to go," I whispered. Catherine, Robin, and I led Tony past the pews, down the center of the chapel, as if a wedding had concluded. Marcie and Rowan were still locked in… whatever it was Marcie was doing on the other side of the pews. Theresa stood between them and us.

When we reached the door, Rowan's head swung toward us and our eyes met. "Get him out of here," I shouted to Catherine. Robin remained by my side, ready to call more energy if needed. Marcie stared at Rowan, likely attempting to reengage her mind manipulation.

"No! You must stop. Why must you refuse to do what is right?" Rowan turned to face me head on, took several steps forward, the edges of her fingertips beginning to crackle. Catherine and Tony were right behind me, at the doorway to the chapel. Steps from safety.

One day I'd learn to manage my smart mouth. Today wasn't that day. "We've won. There's nothing you can do to stop us."

Rowan raised her hands and red energy arced from them, aiming straight for Catherine.

CHAPTER NINETEEN

Action without thought to consequences rarely ends well. I saw the red energy arc from Rowan toward Catherine and without thinking, I dove in front of the empath. The energy from the ghost slammed into me with the burning pain of a thousand suns.

Okay, maybe that was an exaggeration but not much. I slid to the floor, my body in flames. I patted at myself to douse the flames and realized I wasn't on fire. It just felt that way.

"Ow, ow, ow," I said, shocked to discover my words were barely audible. I had thought I was yelling.

A distant voice swam nearer. "Liz! Are you okay?" Catherine's mouth was next to my ear, and I recognized that we had fallen together.

But I didn't care too much. Everything was becoming fuzzy. Fuzzy pain.

I wanted to laugh at the oxymoronic thought, but no longer had the energy.

Something rough touched my cheek and my eyes flew open. Hmm. I didn't know I'd closed them. Images swarmed before me. Tony. Tony licked my cheek. Aww, just like a big kitty. I tried to reach my hand out, but it didn't respond to my command.

Growling penetrated through the fog. That was Tony too. Was he trying to speak to me? I was so tired. And everything hurt so much.

Maybe a quick nap would do the trick. From somewhere in the recesses of my brain, I remembered what I'd learned from television and movies. When severely hurt, if you fell asleep, you died.

The realization sent a shock wave through my body, dulling the pain long enough for me to snap my eyes open again.

Tony stood before me, but facing the other direction. I heard him growling, a constant low rumble. Rowan stood, slack-jawed, staring in our direction, shaking her head. Was she worried my mate would attack her? Was that his plan? Or was he standing guard?

Whimpering reached my ears. Was that me, or Tony? He turned his head, piercing green eyes grabbing mine. He whined again. I could see the human intelligence in there beside the animal. So amazing. I was glad I lived long enough to see it.

With a sigh so small, I doubted anyone noticed, my brain accepted that I was dying. The fiery pain had dimmed to almost nothing. But that seemed to be because I couldn't feel my extremities any longer.

I dropped my head, hoping to catch a glimpse. To see if I even still had extremities. Maybe Rowan had blasted them off, and I was just a stump. That thought ought to terrify me, but didn't.

Hmm. A huge burned gash ran the length of my torso. Good grief, no wonder I thought I was on fire. I wanted to touch the charred edges of my chest, but my arms still weren't responding.

This was what dying felt like. My eyes closed.

Slap! What the—

Someone had smacked me. My eyes fluttered open again, awareness returned. Tony still stood in panther-form, looking back at me, then toward Rowan, back at me again. Catherine's arms came around me, her voice murmured words in my ear that I couldn't comprehend. Robin, Marcie, and Theresa faced Rowan. Robin had her arms raised, as if about to attack. But, why bother? Rowan had won. She'd killed me. The investigation wouldn't go forward.

The timeline would change, just as Rowan wanted. I didn't care anymore. I wanted to sleep. My eyes closed again. Just a little nap. So brief it'd be like it never happened.

Catherine's arms tightened around me and then there was nothing—

CHAPTER TWENTY

Images brightened in my mind. Hmm, was this the last gasp of my brain? Or was I not dying? This seemed like too much awareness for death. But what did I know? I saw Tony, the witches, Catherine, running forward, backward. It was like a movie on fast-forward, then reverse. I frowned. Or tried to. I wasn't sure if my mouth was responding anymore either. Pain flared, then receded, vanished entirely. What on earth?

My eyes widened. The world *was* on fast-forward, then reverse. I glanced down when I felt Catherine's arms tighten, then loosen, then seem to vanish. Holy heck! Her arms *were* tightening, loosening, then vanishing. Her words in my ear came again, then stopped, then came again, but different. Since I hadn't understood her to begin with, I couldn't be sure, but based on what I was seeing, I'd be willing to bet her words were reversed too.

I continued to watch as Catherine's arms phased in and out. I continued to watch as the beings before me zoomed forward and backward. I continued to wince then recover as the pain flared then receded.

Was I in purgatory? Was I stuck in some kind of ghost loop? Destined to relive my dying moment forever? I'd read that in books before, figured if someone created it, in this new world of supernaturals, it was probably possible.

The world froze.

I tried and failed to move, but rather than chalk it up to dying, I assumed I was frozen too. But, why could I hear my thoughts? Why weren't they frozen? This would make an amazing story to tell later.

Catherine's arms tightened around me then loosened.

My eyes closed then reopened. I had the thought that Rowan had won; the timeline would change the way she wanted. Yet, this thought appeared apart from me, running parallel to my current thoughts observing it. Whoa. That was so meta.

Robin's arms were raised as if about to attack Rowan. Marcie and Theresa stood on either side of her.

Catherine's voice murmured in my ear. I again noted my thought that I couldn't comprehend her, running parallel to my observational thought about noticing. She moved backward to stand before me. She was still phasing in and out like she was having trouble staying in our time and/or dimension. My head jerked to the side like someone had slapped me, but then her hand was there on my cheek and my head moved. As if I slapped her hand with my face.

The truth stunned me. Time was moving backward. Yet my thoughts remained enough to observe it.

My eyes closed as time returned to the moment before Catherine slapped me. My eyes opened and looked down to take in the huge burned gash that ran the length of my torso. I had the thought that this was what dying felt like, wanting my arms to respond but they didn't, wanting to touch the charred edges of my chest.

The thought that I was a stump ran through my mind again, my head lay on my chest, trying to determine whether I still had extremities. Then the thought that I couldn't feel my extremities any longer. Dimmed pain began to flare, a breathed out sigh instead of in. Accepting that I was dying.

A thought that I was glad to see Tony's intelligence, then backward into meeting his eyes and seeing the human intelligence beside the animal. He whined again. His electric green eyes moved away from mine and I heard him whimpering. Wondered if that was Tony. Meta-me found this whole reversal fascinating.

Was Tony standing guard or planning to attack Rowan? She stared at me, slack-jawed, then looked away. Tony's growls reached my ears, a constant low rumble. He stood before me, but facing the angry ghost.

Now that I'd realized time was flowing backward, I wondered how far we would go. Back to where Rowan's energy arc hit me? And then what? Move forward again? The thought that I'd spend eternity reliving the most painful moment of my life forever hurt my brain. Was this what it was like for a ghost stuck in a murder-loop?

I re-heard my thought that if you fell asleep when severely injured you died, then my eyes closed. I needed a quick nap. Everything hurt so much. I was so tired. I wondered if Tony was trying to speak to me, then his growling penetrated through my brain fog.

My hand wanted to reach to pet the big kitty, but it didn't respond. Tony's tongue licked my cheek. My eyes closed. Something rough touched my cheek.

Lack of energy prevented me from laughing while I relived my thought about the fuzzy pain. Everything was becoming fuzzy. But I didn't care too much. The meta-me found it interesting that some of this scene flowed the same forward and backward.

I recognized that Catherine was behind me, her mouth next to my ear. "Liz! Are you okay?" Her voice swam away.

When I thought I'd yelled, I was shocked to discover my words were barely audible. "Ow, ow, ow," I repeated.

My body felt like it was on fire. I patted myself to douse the flames, realized I wasn't on fire. I had the strange sensation of sliding *up* from the floor to a standing position. The initial thought of being hit with the burning pain of a thousand suns recurred. And, damn, even in my meta-state, that hurt all over again. But I was still moving. I knew where this would end. My body slid sideways as I reversed my dive in front of Catherine. Rowan's arcing red energy reversed from my chest. So bizarre to see it like it was arcing from me and not to me. It returned to Rowan's hands. The eyes in her face burned with hatred. No, that wasn't right, I realized. It was desperation. That threw meta-me for a moment.

As the energy disappeared into Rowan's hands and she lowered her arms, my mouth moved. Oh, yeah, I had forgotten about my smart aleck comment.

"We've won. There's nothing you can do to stop us," I said backwards.

The world froze again. And then started back up.

Oh no, I'd have to relive the pain again.

Rowan raised her arms to attack, but Catherine was already moving. She leapt toward me and we crashed to the ground as the energy arced harmlessly into the doorjamb behind us. Nobody was hit. Catherine jumped to her feet before I even had time to be awestruck that somehow she reversed time and saved me. Her voice thundered out of her.

"Rowan! Enough. Stop."

And, amazingly, the desperate, time-traveling ghost did.

Everybody halted what they were doing. We all stared at Catherine. Given the looks on the others' faces, I wasn't the only one who just experienced the reversal of that scene. I spoke for all of us.

"Catherine, what the heck just happened?"

CHAPTER TWENTY-ONE

Catherine glanced between all of us, a look of uncertainty on her face. She opened her mouth, closed it.

I jumped into the quiet. "Dang, woman, what did you do? What are you?"

The empath responded to my questions with a quick shake of her head. "I don't know."

"Time went backward. You saved me," I said.

She nodded. "How?"

We all looked around at each other, even Rowan. Nobody had an answer for Catherine. A growl drew my attention and I ran to Tony. I knelt before him, taking his snout into my hands. Those green eyes saw into my soul; that was how it felt, anyway. I kissed the tip of his nose. He chuffed at me, then turned and padded out of the room.

"Tony?" I stepped to follow, but stopped when Marcie shook her head.

"He needs a minute."

Understanding dawned. He needed to shift back into his human form. Hmm, would he be naked when he shifted? A flush crept up my neck at the direction of my thoughts. Hey, that's what happened in the shifter books I read.

Unidentifiable sounds from outside the room reached my ears. What was Tony doing? When he walked back into the room, I couldn't stop the chuckle. He smirked at me.

"Enjoying the show, Liz?" His voice hoarser than normal, perhaps because of the shifting.

"I am," I confirmed. My eyes traveled the length of the now-human shifter. He wasn't naked. It was even better. The noises I'd heard had been him removing a window covering – very *Gone with the Wind*. Tony stood before us with a sheet wrapped, toga style, around his waist, crossing his chest, and over one shoulder. It was a good look on his lithe frame. I wanted to fan myself, but resisted the urge. We exchanged a heat-filled glance. He walked to stand beside me, energy pouring off of him.

Theresa cleared her throat. "Not that this isn't interesting, but what now?" She pointed at the ghost.

All heads swiveled to Rowan. Tears streamed down her face. She shook her head. "I don't understand what happened."

"You killed me," I told her bluntly. "Then Catherine reversed time to undo your damage."

"I don't want to kill anyone," Rowan whispered. Her arms hung at her sides. "I want my family back."

That familiar pain of loss sliced through me at her words. "This isn't the way to do it."

"Maybe I'm wrong?" she asked.

I nodded. "Yeah, I think so."

"What do I do now?"

"I have no idea. We'll help you figure that out." I smiled, and she returned a shy one. I spun to Catherine. "But you… what the heck?"

"I think I know what happened," Rowan answered my question to Catherine.

"You do?" Catherine responded.

"You time traveled," the ghost said simply.

Catherine's mouth fell open. "But… I don't… I've got nothing."

"How is that possible?" Robin asked.

Rowan shrugged. "That I don't know."

"Barbara Knollman said from the moment you came to town that you were important," I reminded Catherine, who blushed.

"Is this what she meant?"

"I have no idea," I answered with a laugh. Adrenaline that had coursed through my body from my near-death experience had made me giddy. "You're going to save the world."

"Not exactly," came a voice from the doorway.

"You do that on purpose, don't you?" I teased the archangel.

"Wouldn't it be boring if I walked in like everyone else?" Olivia Williams responded with a wink.

"Can you explain what Catherine did?" I asked.

The blue-haired, blue-eyed archangel belly laughed. "Of course."

CHAPTER TWENTY-TWO

Catherine, Rowan, Robin, Marcie, Theresa, Tony and I waited semi-patiently for Olivia to deliver on her promise of explaining Catherine's apparent new skill. Time traveling. Who knew?

"First, let me congratulate all of you," Olivia began. "You've done it." She beamed at us.

"Done what? Have we fixed whatever went wrong in Rowan's timeline?" I scratched my head, more like a nervous tic than to show my confusion.

Olivia walked to Rowan, took the time traveling ghost's hands in her own. "Yes," she answered my question, but kept her eyes trained on the ghost. "You have."

Rowan's watery eyes widened and she whispered, "They have?"

Olivia nodded. Rowan threw her arms around the archangel. "Thank you, thank you, thank you." Olivia patted the ghost's head, like comforting a child, before detangling from her.

"It's time for you to return to your own time," Olivia told the ghost.

Rowan grimaced. "You mean, cross over? 'Cause I died."

Olivia quirked an eyebrow. "That's not true anymore."

"It's not?" I asked before Rowan could.

Olivia gestured for me to stay out of it and directed her answer at the ghost. "It's not true anymore," she confirmed. "When I said that the timeline had been changed, I meant completely."

"My family?" Rowan asked, voice trembling.

The archangel nodded. "You're all alive. That's all I can say."

Rowan took several deep breaths. She waved a hand in front of her face but it didn't stop the waterworks. Tears fell and she hugged herself. "I don't know what to say." She looked at the group of us. "I can never repay you."

"I'm glad we did this without anybody dying this time," I quipped, fear rippling through me at my remembered death, though the memory faded more with the passing of time.

Catherine rolled her eyes at me, but said nothing.

"Are you ready?" Olivia asked Rowan.

"Wait!" the ghost exclaimed.

"What?"

"Can you send me back after you explain what Catherine did?"

Olivia's mouth fell open. I guessed it took a lot for someone to surprise her.

"It's just," Rowan continued with a small shrug, "I've never seen a human, even with supernatural abilities, move time back and forth like that." She grinned. "Please."

The archangel chuckled. "Sure. I can do that." Olivia approached Catherine, who dropped her eyes. "Look at me." Catherine complied. "Do you believe you time traveled?"

"That would seem to be the case," she side-stepped in her answer.

"It's not quite accurate."

"It's not?" I interjected again. Olivia ignored me this time.

"What did I do?" Catherine whispered her question. "What am I?"

"You are a descendant of Kronos," Olivia began.

"Wasn't he the God of Time?" Theresa asked.

Olivia nodded. "Yes, he was."

"Catherine's a Goddess?" I asked this incredulously. The empath in question paled. Olivia shook her head.

"It doesn't work like that."

"Thank goodness," Catherine blurted.

"You are genetically a descendant," Olivia clarified.

"What does that mean?" Catherine asked.

"Your role is to keep the timeline on track."

"No pressure there," she muttered.

"When you moved time backward to save Liz, did you consciously choose to do that?"

"No. I didn't even know I could."

"Then what happened?" Olivia asked the question, but I frowned, uncertain where she was going with this line of inquiry.

"Everything felt wrong when Liz died and I had the thought that I needed to fix it." Catherine shrugged. "It all happened so fast."

"In the moment of stress, knowing the timeline was going off track—" Olivia started to say.

"Because Rowan was never supposed to be here," I wondered aloud and Olivia frowned at me for my continual interruptions. I grinned at her. "Sorry."

"Your power activated in that moment of realization," Olivia continued to explain to Catherine. "It didn't matter that you didn't know what was happening."

"I've been in life-threatening situations before. I've had people I care about be in life-threatening situations before—"

"Aw, does that mean you care about me?" I interrupted.

"I'm reconsidering my position on the matter," Catherine said, rolling her eyes.

"Or is it something else that you can't tell us?" I asked Olivia.

"You were partially right, Liz. Rowan was never supposed to be here. But, it was also because it needed to be something messing directly with the timeline to spark the development of the power. Like a trial."

"To see if I was worthy?" Catherine asked.

"Something like that." Olivia tilted her head. "Going forward, you'll become even better at recognizing when things are going sideways and you'll be able to consciously choose to intervene."

Catherine audibly swallowed. "I will? Now that really sounds like a lot of pressure."

"I'll guide you."

"Oh, thank goodness," Catherine breathed.

Olivia turned back to Rowan. "Are you ready now?"

"Yes." The ghost faced us. She appeared stricken. "I want to apologize for all the pain I caused." She looked at me. "Even if some of it was only temporary." Her fingers fidgeted in front of her, clasped together. "I didn't know what else to do. When I discovered I could direct myself elsewhere in time as a ghost, I had to try. I had to save my family." Rowan began glowing. "And I did. Thank you for everything." The ghost flickered, phasing in and out of our dimension, timeline, however Olivia would describe it. With a final wave at us, Rowan winked out of our existence.

Olivia copied Rowan's wave at us. "That's my cue to depart. I'll be in touch," she said to Catherine. "Oh, Liz?"

"Yes?"

"What have you learned from this?"

I frowned. "Don't mess with Catherine?" The empath smacked my arm and the archangel shook her head.

"Try again," she said dryly.

I pondered her question. What was I missing? The heat still flowing off of Tony distracted me for a moment and I gazed at him. He raised his eyebrows. Did he know what the archangel was asking? I turned back to Olivia, lifted my hands in a gesture of helplessness. "I don't know."

Olivia smirked. "Let's just say that you and Tony are more compatible than you might think." And with that obscure pronouncement, Olivia winked out of our existence too.

"That wasn't vague at all," I grumbled.

"We'll give you guys a moment," Catherine said, with a knowing look at us. She and the others filed out, several smiling or waggling their eyebrows at us. When they were gone, I faced Tony.

"Am I the only one who doesn't understand what Olivia was hinting at?"

"Probably."

I slow nodded. "You know what she meant."

"I do."

"And you're not going to tell me."

"I'm not."

"How come?"

Tony didn't answer. He brushed my jaw with his fingers, the touch sending shock waves of pleasure through my body. I curled my fingers around his, holding them in place. Our breath commingled. He stepped back from me, an acute sense of loss filling the space he'd occupied.

"I need to find the answer on my own," I speculated, and he nodded.

"Do you still have reservations about humans and supernaturals?" he asked.

"Yes," I admitted, shame over the answer flooding me. "No matter how much they like and are attracted to each other."

Hurt shown in his eyes, but also compassion and understanding. He gave a sad smile. "At least you admit you find me attractive."

I laughed at the unexpected comment and took a step forward. "Attraction has never been the issue," I assured him. "Time to process. That's what I need," I concluded. "Can you give me that?"

"You know where to find me," he answered. With as much dignity as a man wrapped in a faux-toga could muster, he left the room.

I stood alone and contemplated everything I'd seen, felt, and learned in the past – what? 30 minutes?

When we first met, Tony had been shocked I could smell his cat. Olivia had said he and I were more compatible than I knew. My mind raced. I was fairly certain she didn't mean I was also a shifter, though I poked at my skin anyway.

"Is there an animal under there?" I asked the air.

Receiving no answer, I laughed at myself. All I had right now was my incredible attraction to the sweet, funny, hot, loyal man Tony had shown himself to be in the past few days. Had it only been that short a time? Would that be enough, without knowing the big secret everyone else knew?

The answer rose within me and I smiled. Before I could call Tony to share my revelation, my phone rang.

"Hi, Barbara," I answered. She reminded me that tonight was the vote on the human-supernatural integration bill. "I'll be there as soon as I can get a ride."

CHAPTER TWENTY-THREE

A quick drive from the Arts District to our more-or-less "proper" downtown, and the driver let me off in front of the two-story government building housing the city council. I entered and headed for the marble stairs to the second floor. The preliminaries appeared finished as I snuck in and sat in the audience, wincing when the seat squeaked.

Within the elongated half-circle of elected officials' seats, Mayor Barbara Knollman sat dead-center. Her councilmembers fanned out on either side, every seat taken. No abstentions tonight, I imagined. This was a hot-button issue. Opposite them sat all of us, the audience. Not as filled as I would have expected in the 500-seat occupancy room, but probably a lot more than a typical meeting held. In the center between the audience and the councilmembers was a podium with a microphone. A man stood before it, not speaking. I noticed a line of people behind him. Wow, was this all for the integration bill?

A hand touched my shoulder and a voice whispered in my ear. "Hey, Liz. Long time, no see. I guess you got the call?"

"Hey, guys," I whispered back with a low chuckle, as Catherine, her boyfriend (fiancé?) Alex, Robin, and Marcie filed into the row behind me. Evie the 1920s vampire, her actor boyfriend Ryan, Mia, and her detective boyfriend Jacob had joined them. I gave the group a little wave, noticing the disappointment I felt that Tony hadn't gotten the call, too. Or maybe he needed to check in at the café?

"Thank you all for coming," Barbara's voice cut through my thoughts. "I'm glad to see we have a good turnout for today's historic vote. Most of you know that this afternoon I informed my fellow councilmembers of my intention to introduce new legislation tonight. I wanted them, and the voting public, to be aware of my intention and not feel blind-sided.

"As some of you also know, I went on a local morning show to discuss components of the proposed legislation. I won't repeat that here, except to summarize that the legislation is not the be-all-end-all on the subject. It's an opening round to start the conversation of how to legally integrate human and supernatural societies." She took a sip of water. I knew she couldn't be nervous and figured this was her way of letting the audience catch their breath.

"Before the vote, I'd like to open up the floor for opinions on the proposal. I see folks have already begun lining up." She gestured to the line at the podium. "If you wish to join the queue, please do so." The first gentleman in line stepped up to speak.

"Thank you, Madam Councilwoman," he started, though his voice bounced around the room with strong reverberations. He backed his mouth away, apologizing. "I would like to voice my opposition to the proposal as not having enough safeguards for the human population."

With that salvo, we were off. About a dozen folks spoke, more for the legislation than opposed, I was pleased to see. But, amidst the rhetoric and overblown conclusions, I worried we'd lose the purpose of the legislation.

I made my way toward the podium. Whispers reached me as members of the audience recognized me and commented on my movement. Several folks still in line offered to let me go ahead of them but I declined. That would defeat the purpose of a speech on equal treatment.

When it was my turn, I stepped to the microphone. Barbara lifted a single eyebrow at my presence. "Good evening, councilmembers, concerned citizens, fellow members of the press," I began. "For those of you who do not know me, and for the record," I continued, with a nod toward the woman manning the recording equipment. She smiled up at me. "My name is Elizabeth Addison." I spelled my name. "My job is as a newscaster. For that reason, you may question why I am here, providing my opinion on legislation I will continue to cover." My throat tightened, and I pulled back, coughing to clear it. "I am here, not as a member of the press, but as a citizen of the great city of Las Vegas." A few hearty claps greeted my statement.

"For the past year, humans have learned more and more about the so-called paranormal underworld. Some of that has been negative. A serial killing genie and incubus; homicidal vampire; murdering demon; deadly witch-for-hire; and just this week, an angry time-traveling ghost." Voices tittered at that one. "Don't worry, she's better now," I joked. Laughter rolled through the room.

My gaze traveled up and down the council table. "But those bad apples shouldn't spoil the bunch, to use a trite phrase. Would we want humanity to be judged by the killers among us? Of course not. What I would like for the councilmembers to remember — and the humans who spoke today against the proposal — is that when we keep anyone in the dark, treat anyone like second-class citizens, it goes against everything we stand for.

"This proposal allows us to explore how we live in peace. This proposal allows us to determine what is necessary to manage expectations for beings with, essentially, superpowers. This proposal is a step forward, allowing all beings equal treatment under the law." I waited for the spontaneous applause that erupted to stop.

"Thank you very much for your time, councilmembers, and I hope that you vote with your conscience." To more thunderous applause, and a few boos, I retook my seat with my friends, only half of whom were human, I realized with an internal chuckle. A few more citizens spoke for and against the proposal. Then it was time for the vote.

A hush settled over the room. The seven members of the council, including the mayor, leaned forward to speak a single word when their names were called. As each "aye" rang out over the crowd, tears pricked my eyes. The proposal passed unanimously. I heard the doors at the back of the auditorium open, most likely as members of the press raced out to film quick shots to notify their viewers of the proposal's passage.

In the room, a motion was made to adjourn, it was seconded, and the meeting ended. Just like that, they had charted a new path forward. Exciting times to be a citizen, a member of the press, and a potential romantic interest of a supernatural.

People rose and began filing out. I caught up with Catherine.

"Well?" I asked, raising an eyebrow.

"Well, what?" She played dumb.

I laughed. "Fine, don't tell me."

She leaned forward, her lips an inch from my right ear. "I told him yes. We'll announce wedding details when we make them."

With a squeal, I threw my arms around her and gave a thumbs up to Alex, who just shook his head with a laugh. Those involved with the Rowan event knew, but others glanced at me in confusion.

For the first time in my life as a newscaster, I didn't desire to explain. It wasn't my story to tell.

I had my own story to tell in the morning. And I had a lot to say.

CHAPTER TWENTY-FOUR

Marilyn cocked an eyebrow at me. "You seem nervous, Liz." She leaned forward to apply blush to my cheeks. "What gives?"

"I'm going out on a limb with this morning's show."

She smirked. "Don't you do that every other day or so?"

I laughed. "Touché." My eyes closed so she could apply the setting powder over my entire face. When she finished, I continued. "But, seriously, this one is more… personal."

"Oh? Maybe I'll watch then."

"Don't put yourself out," I said. She laughed.

"Have a good show." With that, she left the room. I confirmed I looked camera-ready and then headed for the studio. The production assistant hadn't come to get me yet, but I was ready. In every sense of the word.

"Liz, I was just coming to get you," the PA said when I met her in the hallway.

"Let's rock this thing," I responded, and we continued to the studio.

After taking my seat on the familiar stuffed blue chair and crossing my legs, I watched the teleprompter above the camera scroll backward and forward to finally land on my opening for the show. Not that I needed it. Not this time. I had my entire speech memorized. I hadn't been exaggerating when I told Marilyn this one was personal. Even when I'd invited the murderous genie into my home for an interview – that hadn't gone quite as planned – that was still business. This would definitely veer into personal.

The countdown to the start sounded in my ear. I cleared my throat and prepared to speak.

Camera rolling sounded in my ear bud, I opened my mouth, and nothing came out. With a deep breath, I nodded as though this was business-as-usual and tried again. Words emerged. Thank goodness.

"Good morning in the Valley! Welcome to *Entertainment Daily*, Las Vegas' most watched morning show. I'm your host, Elizabeth Addison." My smile dropped for a moment. "For those viewers keeping count, I'm still alive and today is Day 4. If you remember, several days ago, a time-traveling ghost bent on changing the future told me I had three days to live. That worked out pretty well in the end." I gave a quick summary of what had happened.

"Once we saved the future," I said with a chuckle, "it was time to take steps to put us on that path. I'm pleased to report, for those who missed the sweeping coverage last night, Mayor Knollman's integration legislation passed unanimously at the City Council meeting last night. Congratulations, Barbara." I cleared my throat again. Here came the challenging part.

"Last night, I voiced my support for this legislation. It was both political support and personal support. Over the course of the last year, I've made many supernatural friends. They've saved my hide, figuratively and literally. They deserve equal treatment."

I could hear my blood thundering in my brain. I hoped I didn't have a stroke from the nerves. "My friends know that I've expressed concern that humans and supernaturals were too different, the challenges too great to overcome, to make a romantic relationship work. Well, they may have an extra layer of challenge, but I've seen it work." I winked at the camera, hoping Catherine and Alex were watching the broadcast.

"And I've recently met a very special supernatural. If he's still willing to take a chance on an insecure, uncertain human, I'd like to have a chat." My mouth felt like I stuffed it with cotton balls, and I wished I'd thought to put a cup of water on the table beside me. "We'll take a break for some words from our sponsors and be right back."

The rest of the show passed in a blur. Everyone congratulated me when I left the studio and walked past the cubicles to my glass-walled office. I closed the door, sank into my desk chair, and with a tremulous breath, withdrew my cellphone from the top drawer. A text message.

Please come by the café when you have time.

Heart in my throat I replied. *On my way.*

CHAPTER TWENTY-FIVE

Butterflies had taken flight in my belly. I took several deep calming breaths before opening the door to Tony's café. Why was I nervous? He'd dropped enough hints of his interest and I finally got my priorities aligned. This would be fine.

Tony's eyes lit up when he saw me, and I knew I'd made the right decision. He stepped toward me as I crossed to the counter. "Hey there, stranger," I greeted the were-panther.

"I saw your show this morning," he responded. He started to rest his arms on the countertop, reversed motion, and stepped around and out toward me. His familiar heat rolled off him, warming me.

"What did you think?"

"I liked it."

"I'm glad."

Tony took my hands in his. "What changed?"

Squeezing his hands, I grinned. "I got out of my own way," I quipped before answering for real. "Seriously? I thought about how I feel when I'm around you." He smiled lasciviously and I shook my head with a chuckle. "I considered how I feel when I'm not around you." His smiled dropped. "I thought about your reaction when I could smell your cat—"

"Panther," he corrected, but his smile was back in place.

"Panther," I agreed with a good-natured eye roll. "I considered what Olivia said about our compatibility." My eyes met his, unshed tears blurring my view of him. I blinked to clear the image. "When you were hurt," I swallowed as the remembered pain passed through me, "I thought of you as my... mate."

Tony gasped and tightened his grip on my hands. "What does all that mean?"

"I'm not certain. I'm not a shifter, but I can sense the shifterness of you," I teased him. "It doesn't matter if I'm human. I want to be with you. None of the rest of it matters."

Tony's eyes dilated and he leaned toward me, releasing my hands so he could cup my face. He feathered delicate kisses on my forehead, my cheeks, my nose (that triggered a giggle from me). We'd only met four days ago; it was like the insta-attraction in a romance novel.

But it was real.

His chapped lips found mine. Gentle at first, then with more passion. Energy zinged through me and my arms wrapped around him, pulling him closer. My heart swelled with... surely not love yet, but something similar...

I pulled back and smirked.

"What?" he asked, his sexy voice pitched low.

I stood on my toes, leaned forward again. My lips stopped an inch from his ear. "If you know what Olivia meant, will you tell me now?" I whispered.

Tony chuckled. "I wasn't positive until you said you thought of me as your mate," he began to explain, his eyes shining with that same undefined feeling. "You carry shifter genes—"

"No way," I interrupted in an exclamation that drew the attention of the few people in the café who weren't already watching our performance. My head dropped onto his shoulder. A flush crept across my face.

He lifted my chin to regain eye contact. "Yes way." He beamed. "And you probably can carry shifter offspring."

After I picked my jaw up off the floor, I responded to his bombshell. "That's a conversation for another time."

"Indeed."

I placed my hands on his chest, reveling in the warmth and strength pulsing under my palms and fingers. "Guess this is the dawn of the Age of the Supernaturals."

"That's not dramatic at all," Tony teased. "Like this is a television show."

"Don't you want there to be a season two?"

"You mean, after this exciting season finale?"

"Exactly. This doesn't have to be the end. We want people to tune in again."

"I'm not sure I could take the excitement," Tony said drily.

A giggle bubbled up. I wrapped my arms around his middle again, looked up into his amazing chocolate brown eyes. "How about being my date for a friend's wedding then?"

His lips closed on mine again and his nod moved my head in concert. I tried not to giggle, but another escaped around our clasped lips. "This is going to be so much fun," I whispered.

"Yes, it will, my mate."

EPILOGUE

I told myself I wouldn't cry, but tears formed when I saw Catherine in the open doorway of the chapel room, in her simple white knee-length fitted sheath, blond hair falling loose around her shoulders. Elvis stood next to her, guitar at the ready. He strummed the strings, and the two began to walk down the short aisle.

A hand took mine, and I glanced into Tony's face. He leaned over to kiss my cheek. We both turned to watch the bride continue down the aisle, the good-looking young Elvis singing a love song. I shifted my gaze to Alex, looking sharp in a black tuxedo, standing at the altar with the wedding officiant, a tall, thin, older man with an engaging smile.

Catherine reached her groom. Her blue eyes mirrored the happy tears in his green ones. Alex took her hands in his. The grins on their faces sparked many in the audience.

"Friends and family, welcome," the officiant began. Although, to be accurate, it was mostly Paranormal Talent Agency friends. I chuckled when I realized how many of us had found love, thanks to Catherine accepting the job opportunity of starting the West Coast arm of the Peterson Talent Agency here in Las Vegas. And how many of us weren't even human.

"We are gathered here today to witness the joining of Catherine and Alex." I wasn't big on ceremonies, so my attention drifted. I glanced around at the group sitting in cushioned folding chairs arranged like pews.

Vampire Evie, her 1920s blond bob in place, snuck looks at her human boyfriend Ryan, his auburn hair in need of a trim. Nixie Mia, her green hair in an elaborate French braid, held hands with her human boyfriend Jacob, his close-cut blond hair not in need of a trim. Robin and Jackson, human witches, their heads resting against each other. And, even Barbara and Liam, 500-year-old angels, recently reunited.

I refocused on the couple at the altar as the officiant reached the question-and-answer portion of the ceremony.

"Do you, Catherine Rodham, promise to love and trust Alex, in sickness and in health, in adversity and prosperity, for better or worse, so long as you both shall live?"

"I do." She smiled, happiness radiating off of her. I'd swear she was glowing. Now that we knew she was descended from a god, maybe she was.

"Do you, Alexander Moore, promise to love and trust Catherine, in sickness and in health, in adversity and prosperity, for better or worse, so long as you both shall live?"

"I do." He blew her a kiss and she giggled.

"Do you have the rings?"

Catherine and Alex answered yes. Mia and Jacob handed the rings over, unadorned platinum bands.

"With this ring, I thee wed," Catherine spoke softly.

"With this ring, I thee wed," Alex echoed.

And then the moment we were waiting for.

"By the authority given me by the State of Nevada, I now pronounce you man and wife," the officiant intoned. "You may kiss your bride."

Alex scooped Catherine up in his arms – not easy to do when she was so tall – yet delivered a chaste kiss. His lips moved, and I wondered what he was saying, but glad that they would have those whispered words to themselves.

Elvis began playing something fast, and the newlyweds walked back down the aisle to where Catherine had entered. They beamed as they passed their assembled friends.

All brought together by the Paranormal Talent Agency and leading the charge into the Age of the Supernaturals. Catherine and Alex disappeared through the doorway. Elvis stopped walking but continued singing. We in the audience waited with bated breath. The newlyweds reappeared back in the doorway, we whooped our appreciation, and then everyone was standing, hugging, declaring ecstatic congratulations to the couple.

We'd all done it.

Happily ever after.

THANK YOU!

Thank you so much for supporting my work and reading this book. I truly hope you enjoyed reading it as much as I did writing it.

If you liked the book, please consider leaving a review online.

Just a few lines would be great. Reviews are not only the highest compliment you can pay to an author, they also help other readers discover and make more informed choices about purchasing books in a crowded online space. Thank you so much in advance.

If you didn't like the book or have concerns, please email me directly at
heather@heathersilvio.com

ABOUT THE AUTHOR

Heather has written fiction and nonfiction; she is also an actress and licensed psychologist. When she isn't working, she channels her inner flapper as a 1920s jazz and blues singer.

Visit http://www.heathersilvio.com for more information and to sign up for her New Releases and Appearances Newsletter.

9 781732 693890